the Øffenders

Saving the world while serving detention!

by JERRY CRAFT
with Jaylen craft
and aren craft

www.jerrycraft.net
jerrycraft@aol.com

Mama's Boyz, Inc • Norwalk

PUBLISHER'S NOTE: This is a work of fiction. Names, characters, places, and incidents are either the product of the authors' brilliant imaginations or are used fictitiously, and any resemblance to actual persons, living, dead or undead; events, or locales is entirely coincidental. So there!

Publisher's Cataloging-In-Publication Data (Prepared by The Donohue Group, Inc.)

Craft, Jerry.
   The offenders : saving the world while serving detention! / by Jerry Craft, with Jaylen Craft and Aren Craft.

   p. : ill. ; cm.

   Summary: A freak accident gives five middle school bullies super powers. But instead of being able to transform into cool super-beings, they take on the characteristics of the kids who they pick on. Sure, their abilities may be at an all-time high, but do they really have what it takes to save their school when their self-esteem is at an all-time low?
   Common Core State Standards reading literature strands: RL.6.1,2,3,4,5,6,9,10; RL.7.1,2,3,4,6,10; RL.8.1,2,3,4,6,10.--Supplied by publisher.
   Interest grade level: 5-8.
   ISBN-13: 978-0-9796132-7-2
   ISBN-10: 0-9796132-7-2

   1. Bullying--Juvenile fiction. 2. Superheroes--Juvenile fiction. 3. Self-esteem--Juvenile fiction. 4. Bullies--Fiction. 5. Superheroes--Fiction. 6. Self-esteem--Fiction. I. Craft, Jaylen. II. Craft, Aren. III. Title.

PZ7.C734 O34 2014
[Fic]   2013915262

The Offenders text, cover art and illustrations copyright ©2014 Mama's Boyz, Inc.
Book design by Danni Ai courtesy of DACCo Multimedia, Inc;
Jaylen and Aren Craft produced by Autier and Jerry Craft ©2014
Special thanks to Ernestine Eisenhauer, Greg Amos, Eric Velasquez; Deb Strait; Cathy Bonczak; Carrie Smith; Trisha Barron; Jeanne White; Drew Pearce; Alex Roehner; DoSomething.org; Angela Weigle; and Steven Shuchat, Theresa Chirico, Allyson Rubin & the rest of my friends at Van Wyck J.H.S.

Visit us on the Web! www.jerrycraft.net or email: jerrycraft@aol.com Follow me on Facebook, Twitter, and all those other places.

Printed and bound in the United States of America
10 9 8 7 6 5 4 3 2 1

Mama's Boyz, Inc
304 Main Ave #114
Norwalk, CT 06851
info@mamasboyz.com

"Knowing what's right doesn't mean much unless you DO what's right."

Theodore Roosevelt

OUR LUNCH LADY ISN'T USUALLY THIS GREEN!

Chaos! That's the only word that describes my school right now! And I don't mean, *like*, the usual chaos that goes on here at *William Shatner Middle School*. This is bad ... real bad! I'm standing in "the big circle." That's the place where our parents come to pick us up or drop us off. (Except for Kimmy, who makes her mom drive around back.) Well, I'm not really standing, I'm hiding. Hiding for my life! That's because I'm so scared that I don't know what else to do!

My principal can't help me because he got tied up when this all started. And even if he wasn't tied up, I doubt there's anything that he could do. The same goes for my friends — I never thought I'd call them *that* — they're not much better off. Bobby's not moving at all. That can't be good. Dexter doesn't look so good either. Same for Kimmy. And if Buck isn't cracking jokes, then he *must* be in bad shape, too. Like I said, this is bad ... real bad!

If I told you everything that has happened today, you'd call me crazy. Heck, I'd even call me crazy. But that's how my life is these days. Ever since ... well, I'll tell you more when I think you can handle it. But all I can tell you now is that my friends need my help and I don't know what to do. Everyone thinks that I'm so tough, but right now, I'm one big fat chicken!

"I'll bet you'll all listen to me now," says a voice breaking through the silence. It makes my hair stand up on the back of my neck. I start to sweat some more, and that ache in my belly gets bigger.

"You'll listen to me real good now, *won'tcha*?" she says again. That's Miss Mary, she works here. Well, she used to, before she destroyed the school. I doubt they'll let her keep her job now. She looks around the circle to see if there are any more kids around. There aren't! I think most of them are hiding in the gym. I wish I was with them.

She moves around the circle really slowly, floating about three feet off the ground. Yeah, that's right, I said "floating." That's what I was talking about. Weird, right? The sunlight brings out the *greenish* tint to her skin. I know you don't know her, but she's usually not that color. I look around to see if someone is coming to help us. Nope. All I see is lots of food scattered all over the ground. Chicken nuggets, hot dogs ... you name it. It looks like a fast-food joint threw up on our school. I can't even, *like*, call the police because there's no cell phone service here. Not that I could use my phone anyway. And you wouldn't be able to either, if you were only *six-inches tall!*

Okay, I think I'm, *like*, ready to share our story now, but don't say I didn't warn you. It all started not too long ago ...

Flip the pages and watch what happens to this picture:

MINA MADSEN: QUEEN OF FOUR-SQUARE

— by Mina Madsen

My name is Mina, and this is, *like*, my favorite part of the school day, and my favorite place to be — recess at the four-square court! For those of you who have never heard of four-square, where have you been, hiding under a rock?! It's only, *like*, the *most awesome* game in the history of the whole world! It should definitely be an Olympic sport instead of some of those lame ones they have now — like skating, track, swimming ... Jeez, who watches that stuff anyway? And there should be, *like*, a professional four-square league where kids like me could grow up and make millions of dollars. I can see myself as the star of my college team, then turning pro. Then I'd get to do Nike commercials, and a whole bunch of others ... Gatorade, Foot Locker ... you name it. My face would be plastered all over everywhere. I'd be like LeBron. Only a girl, *and* more famous, of course!!

So here's how you play four-square: first you draw a great big square on the ground. I don't know exactly how big, *like*, maybe ten feet by ten feet, who knows? Then you split it into four smaller boxes. You could use chalk, but then you'd have to redo it every time it rains. Luckily the courts here at school are painted on the ground. The first box is called *A-square*; that probably stands for *awesome*. It's the only square worth being in, and it's the only place where you get to serve from. Now the one to your left is called *B-square*, as in *boring*. Then *C-square* and *D-square*. Now the cool part about being in *A-square*, besides the fact that that's usually where you'll find me, is not only do you get to serve, but you get to make all the rules. Personally I like *double taps*, *holds*, *outs-on-serves* and *snake eyes*. There are tons of others, too: *body parts*, *chicken feet* ... but most are pretty lame. I don't have time to explain them all to you, but I'm sure you can go look it up online or somewhere. Here, let me draw you a picture. See? That's me in *A-square*.

Now the next thing you need is a ball. One of those big-rubber-bouncy balls is best. Like the kind you use to play kick ball. It's the size of a soccer ball, but a lot softer. You don't want it to be too hard 'cause then you'll hurt your hands. Most of them are either blue or red and sometimes even

green or purple. I like the red ones best. Now once you serve, the game is basically like tennis with four people, except you hit the ball with your hands. Unless some freak calls *body parts* (which I hate), that means you can, *like*, hit the ball with your feet or your head or whatever. Lame, right? Then, whoever gets out, goes all the way back to *D-square*. Unless there are a bunch of *dweebs* waiting to play, then they go to the back of the line. I call it the "losers line." Now if you'll excuse me, I have some business to take care of. Math class was particularly boring today, so I need a little extra excitement. Plus my sister was a real *pain in the butt* on the way to school this morning, which was *very* stressful for me. I think she accidentally stabbed herself in the leg with a pencil or something. Whatever! I didn't bother to ask, but it looked like it hurt. The point is, I have plenty of steam that I need to let out. And who better to let it out on than Meagan Stevens? I, *like*, absolutely *hate* her!

Now all great athletes have a ritual, here's mine: I start by slipping off my red flip-flops and putting them over on the grass so no one steps on them. Then I take off one of the three red hair bands that I wear on my right wrist and use it to tie my hair up so it doesn't get in my eyes. I pull the little feather that I wear in my hair down because I like that to swing when I play. I bet you can guess what color it is. Red! Then I twist my ring around on my finger so the little black stone part is tucked safely inside my fist to keep it safe when I slam the ball. The last thing I do is tug on the friendship bracelet (that I wear on my left wrist) three times for good luck. I made it myself out of red duct tape. It's pretty cool if I do say so myself. I made a matching case for my iPod too.

Now I'm ready for business. I look around to see who's in each square. Dana is in *B-square*, but, *like*, she's not much of a threat. Sam is in *C*, he's not that great either. But Meagan is in *D-square*. The longer I leave her in, the more chances she'll have to get me out. That means she has to go! And fast!!!

"Okay, losers, you know *my* rules," I say while bouncing the ball.

By the way, unless you call *crazy serves*, then you have to hit it to the person diagonally across from you in *C-square*, or, as I call it, "Crappy-square." Luckily I already know that if I hit it to Sam, he'll hit it right back to me. He's so, *like*, predictable. So that's what I'll do. *Oops*, I almost forgot to take off my new necklace so I don't snap it by accident. It's *so* pretty! It's really delicate and has a little heart charm that's made of real gold. I'd hate for anything to happen to it. I undo the clasp and gently coil it up and wrap it in a tissue before I place it in my pocket. Then I put on my game face to show these losers that I mean business. Deep breath … Here's my serve:

Bop …

Perfect! Nice and soft, so even an *epic fail** like Sam should have no problem hitting it back to me. Meagan however, won't be so lucky because before Sam hits it back to me, I get in the perfect spot to slam the ball right at her! If I'm lucky, which I will be (actually, it's more skill than luck), I'll get her out. But if I'm *really* lucky, I'll, *like,* get her out *and* be able to bounce the ball off her big, fat head. That would be just perfect! Remind me one day to tell you all about the day that I gave Nick a black eye. I wish I had that on video, I'd watch it over and over. Or even better, I'd put it up on YouTube. I'd bet it would go viral like one of those stupid cat videos. Now at recess, Nick plays tetherball.

Sam lobs it back to me, just as planned, and I draw back my arm to deliver the crushing blow …

BAM!!!

Oh, what a thing of beauty! It shoots by Meagan without her even touching it. She's out! Then the ball rolls, *like,* all the way to the fence. Now she has to take "the wimp's walk." That's when everyone stops and watches as she, *like,* walks to go get the ball. That's it, keep rolling … make her walk all the way to the fence. I take this time to see who's next on line. Marina. Oh please! No real threats in this round. So, like I always say, when in doubt, pick on a boy. As the ball gets closer to the space in the fence, Meagan starts to run 'cause if she doesn't get it in time, *like,* the ball could roll through and go all the way to the main entrance of the school. That would be good … real good. Come on, roll … roll.

Dang! … She got it. Oh well, time to take Sam out.

Maybe I can bounce the ball off of *his* head.

*Check out the definition of *epic fail* in the back of the book.

9

1 ½

SAM "NOSE" BEST

— by Mina Madsen

I've been sitting here on the ground for, *like*, the last ten minutes twisting my ankle bracelet while the school nurse applies pressure to Sam's nose to stop the bleeding. Boy, what a gusher! I must have hit it harder than I thought. Oh well, I guess Nick just got himself a new tetherball partner. As soon as the nurse takes him back to her office, I hop up and yell "okay girls, let's play!"

"B-but there's blood in *C-square,* says Jenna Parker, who, by the way I *also* hate.

"What's the matter, Jenny, afraid of a little blood?" Oooh, *zing*! I am *on fire* today.

"My name is Jenna! Jen-NA, not Jenny. You know, you have the perfect name ... Mina. 'Cause no one is *meaner* than you!"

"Like that's the first time I ever heard *that* lame joke! Besides I *kinda* like it. Maybe I'll put it on a T-shirt. You're just mad because I'm better than you at four-square," I shot back. She knows she had better not mess with me because I can ... oh ... what's this? ... Are her eyes getting a little shiny? *Yep*, sure looks like it. And her little lips are, *like*, starting to quiver. Poor little baby mouse, looks like the dam's about to burst.

So here's the difference between me and other kids. See another kid would, *like*, see that she's about to cry and let her off the hook. But then, she might come back another day and try to stand up to me again. And who knows, maybe she'll catch me one day when I'm not prepared. Hey, it happens to the best of us. My mom always says that, "when you see an enemy showing signs of weakness, that's the time to strike even harder." She's a big-time lawyer, you know.

Now the way to make sure that someone *never* messes with you again is to embarrass them in front of a big group. The bigger the group, the better. Especially if, *like*, there are a bunch of dumb boys around, because they're so immature that they laugh at anything. And not only do they laugh loud, but it takes them, *like*, ten minutes to *stop* laughing. They're like a pack of hyenas. Then *they're* the ones who the teachers get mad at. Not me. Genius, right? So I look Jenny right in her red, watery eyes and say loud enough for the entire playground to hear:

"Well, JENNY, if my name fits me, then your mom *shoulda* named you MOUSEY, 'cause that's what *you* are, a defenseless little mouse!"

Ouch! She won't be returning that insult just like Sam couldn't return my slam. Well it's like they say, "recess is war!" Actually, I've never heard anyone else say that, but that doesn't mean that I can't be the first!

"I ... I hate you, Mina! You wear that stupid shirt that says 'Love' but no one even likes you! You always have to make people feel so *small!* That's why you don't get invited to parties or sleepovers," she said running into the building with tears flying everywhere. Boy, they're really *gonna* have to clean *C-square* good tonight. All it needs now is for someone to wet their pants and it will have just about every bodily fluid you can think of.

"You can go hang out with Sam in the nurse's office!" I yelled as the door closed behind her. "Tell her you have a wounded ego! Maybe she'll even put a bandage on it." *Ugh!* That Jenny is the worst. She's like a little baby sometimes. Half the time you don't even know she's around. And now when it finally comes time to stand up for herself, she cries and runs off like a mouse when you turn on the lights. *Wimp!*

"Okay, can we finally start playing again?" I yell out. Now let's see. Dana is still in "Boring-square," Christopher is now in "Crappy-square" and Hannah is in "Dummy-square." And at this rate, by the time Meagan gets to the front of the line again, recess will be over. Which is great, because she's, *like*, my only real competition anyway.

"You know the rules, girls."

"Hey!" says Christopher, "I'm a boy."

"If you say so," I shoot back. I have to start writing this stuff down!

BOP!

I serve the ball to Christopher who uses both hands to hit it over to Dana who hits it back to him. Then he hits it to Hannah, who also hits it back to him. This happened a few times before it dawned on me that they were *freezing* me out! They're too chicken to hit the ball to me, because they all know that I'll get them out. I can't believe it. What a bunch of cheaters!!! I'll bet Meagan put them up to it. Where is she? Boy, I'm *gonna* shoot her the nastiest, dirtiest, *most angriest* look ever. I stare over in her direction until she looks back at me. Then I look directly into her beady-little-eyes. She looks good and scared ... Then all of a sudden, her eyes open big as watermelons and I hear:

"YOU'RE OUT!!!" yelled Dana.

Omigosh! They hit it to me when I wasn't paying attention!

"That's not fair, I wasn't looking!"

Then all at once everyone starts screaming and laughing. And it's at ME!

"But, *like*, I wasn't looking!"

"Doesn't matter, you're *still* out!" says Christopher.

"*LIKE*, maybe next time, *LIKE*, you'll keep your eyes on the ball instead of, *LIKE*, shooting dirty looks at people!" adds Meagan. "*LIKE LIKE LIKE*! That's the only word you know! Which is funny because nobody *LIKES* you!"

All of a sudden, the hyenas roared with laughter! But, wait, they're not supposed to be laughing at *me!* They're *my* hyenas!!!

"Line!" I said, "The ball was on the line!!!" I said again while pointing down to the ground.

Of course Meagan was the first one to respond with, "No it wasn't. Besides, how could you even see the ball when you were looking at *me* the whole time, *Mean-a*? Why don't you just put your little red flip flops back on and leave? No one wants to see your dirty little feet anyway!"

"Do over!" I yelled even louder and folded my arms to show that I

wasn't about to move.

"NO!" It was like every kid on the playground said it at the same time. It was like they had been rehearsing it for one of our stupid school plays or something. Oh, this really stinks! But Mina Madsen *never* goes down without a fight! I went one by one, starting with Dana, and said every mean thing I could think of. I talked about their clothes, their hair, their fat heads, I even said some stuff about Clay's dog. Stupid little dog, he thinks it's *soooooooo* adorable. But it's a mutt. If I had a dog it would be a pure breed. Like the kind you see at that Westmin-i-ster Dog Show or whatever it's called.

I was saving my best insults for Meagan, though. I was *gonna* get her good, but then the weirdest thing happened. All of a sudden, she starts laughing. Then so does everyone else. They must have all gone crazy at the same time. So I just looked at them trying to figure out what was so *dog-gone* funny. Suddenly I felt someone standing behind me. Close. Real close. I bet it's Sam who finally came back from the nurse's office and is now holding bunny ears over my head. Well if he thinks his nose hurt before, it's about to hurt a whole lot more now, because I plan to bounce the ball off of it again. So before he can get away, I pick up the ball and spin in one move. Then I throw it as hard as I can right where his fat head should be.

KA-POW!!!

I nailed him! What a throw!

Well ... it would have been perfect ... except for the fact that it wasn't Sam who was behind me. It was Principal Marshkin. And it wasn't his nose that I *bopped* him in. It was lower. Much lower. Much *much* lower.

Uh-oh!

He looked up at me while kneeling on one knee and slowly opened his mouth to say something. Shoot, this isn't going to be good.

"D ... d ... detention!" he whispered.

This is bad ... real bad!

2

2 KOOL 4 SKOOL!
— by Dexter Diaz

Dex

My name is Dexter Diaz, Jr. But you can call me Dex. I hate school! You know, *bro*, it's *like* why do I *hafta* waste my time getting a so-called education when I already know that I want to be a mechanic in my dad's auto shop? He owns it with his cousin Hector. I mean, *you know*, what good is learning geometry and stuff when all I'll need to know is how to fix cars and motorcycles?

So anyway, I'm counting down the minutes *'til* class ends. We got our homework back and I got a B+. But there's also a note at the top of the page that says, "see me after class." Man, that can't be good. Unless Miss Brea wants to tell me that I did a good job. I hope she doesn't expect me to do this all the time now.

Finally the bell rings! All the kids get up to go to their next classes like a herd of cattle. Not me, what's the rush? As they go through the door, Principal Milkman squeezes past them and heads over to Miss Brea's desk. They talk for a minute or so, then she gives me that one finger "come here" gesture. I take a deep breath, jam my notebook in my backpack, then head up to see what they want. Hopefully they're waiting to congratulate me. Maybe they like my new sneakers. I *do* look pretty good today.

"Please take off your sunglasses," says Principal Milkman.

Man, they never let me keep these on. My *shades* are my trademark, like my red sweatshirt that I keep zipped up all the way to the top. I like the way it fits around my chin. Makes me look like Iron Man. But I know I can't win this fight, so I slide my shades up to the top of my head.

"A B+, Dexter, this is the best paper you've handed in all year," says Miss Brea.

Cool, they're both smiling. I guess this is *gonna* be a happy speech after all. "Well, I tried really hard," I said.

"That's nice. However, it's not that we don't think you're *capable* of doing this type of work all the time, Dexter ..." she said.

"That's *Dex*," I interrupted.

"Yes ... Well, like I was saying, it's not that we don't think you're *capable* of doing this type of work all the time, uh ... Dex, we just don't feel like you did it *this* particular time."

"You mean, it *ain't* good?" I asked.

"No, it's *not* good" she responded.

"So how could it not be good, you gave me a B+?" See that's what I mean about school. That just doesn't make sense now, you know?

"No, no, I mean it's *not* good, not it *ain't* good," she said.

"Wait, I'm confused, is it *not* good, or *ain't* it good?" I asked shrugging my shoulders.

"It's not, *ain't* good, Dexter, it's just *not* good," she answered again.

"It's Dex," I corrected again. "So if it *ain't* good, how come you gave me a B+?!!" I asked again. Man, now I'm getting upset!

"Wait, let's start over … This paper is very good, Dexter … uh … Dex. We just don't feel like you're the one who wrote it."

Oh man, I was right, this *ain't* good! Guess I won't be getting the happy speech after all. Man, all of a sudden, their faces both changed from smiles to frowns. It's like the end of the first *Raiders of the Lost Ark* movie where that ghost-thing looks like an angel at first, then … *boom* … all of a sudden it gets all evil-looking and stuff. I watched it on cable recently. Not bad for an old movie. It got an 8.7 on IMDB.com.

"What? Just *'cause* it's good, you don't think that I could do it?" I asked, trying to put them on the defensive. "That's racist, *bro!*"

"No, Dex, we don't think you did it, for a few reasons. For one, this report was printed on stationery with the initials H. P. on it. Now what do you suppose that stands for?"

"*Ummm ...* Hewlett Packard?" I asked softly. "Yeah, that's what it stands for," I added with more confidence. "That's the paper that came with my printer and I wanted to use it up."

"I see," she sighed. "I was thinking more that the initials stood for Hayden Parker."

"*Shoot no*, why would you think that?"

"Well, Dexter ... I mean, Dex ... I'm glad you asked. If you hold the paper up to the light and look under this mound of Wite-Out, you can see Hayden Parker's name." Looks like someone, and I'm assuming that someone is *you*, covered up his name and wrote your name next to it in pen. The rest of the paper was typed on a computer, I might add."

Ooohhh. You know, I *gotta* keep this stuff in mind next time I get someone to do my homework for me.

Man, Miss Brea is smarter than I gave her credit for. They got all "C.S.I." on me. Next they'll be dusting for fingerprints. I guess if this was one of those cop shows on TV, this would be the part where I would demand to see my lawyer. I'm in big trouble and there's nothing I can do about it. The more I lie, the more trouble I'll get in. Wish I was a girl right now so I could start crying. I know that sounds racist. No, wait, not racist — What's the other one? Well, you know what I mean. Maybe that would help. But if the other kids saw me *bawlin'* like that, all my years of being cool would disappear just like that.

So instead, I just looked over at Principal Milkman, who, up *'til* now hadn't said much. I may not be smart, but I'm smart enough to know that he's about to say just one word. And I'll bet that one word is ...

"Detention?" I asked.

"Detention," he answered.

'sta loca!*

---

* Check out the meaning in the *"A Little Bit From Dex"* page in the back of the book.

3

THE "TOOTH" HURTS
— *by Buck Bievers*

"Hey, *brace face!* How *'bout lettin'* me cut the line?"

"Get lost, Buck," answered Grace as she stood near the front of the line. Today they're serving pizza, which is my favorite food in the whole world. So I don't really feel like getting on the back of the line. Now if it was *Sloppy Joe day*, I wouldn't just be glad to get on the back of the line, I'd insist on it! I know some kids say they like it, but personally, I think it's gross. Sweet meat. *Yuck!* Who came up with that recipe? Let's see … first start out with meat, doesn't matter what kind … maybe monkey meat … coyote meat … whatever … then add some sugar and stir … *Done!*

I continue, "Don't you think it's a bit of a *co-inky-dink* that your name is Grace, which rhymes with brace … and you've got them all over your face? You should get a t-shirt that says *'brace-face Grace.'* What do you think about that?" I asked.

"And don't *you* think it's a *co-inky-dink* that your hair is *curly* and you look all *girly*?" she shot back at me.

"Ha, ha, ha," I laughed sarcastically. What people don't realize is being funny is an art. And it's an art that I take quite seriously. Hey that's funny, taking laughter seriously. See that's what I mean, I can be funny even when I'm not trying. It's a gift! Not everyone can make people laugh. But I don't do it with the stupid kid-stuff. You know, kids who just say words like *booger* or *fart* so that all the immature kids fall over laughing or squirt milk *outta* their noses. Yo, *my* stuff is clever!

"Hey, Grace, with teeth like yours, if you were a singer, you'd be Justin BEAVER!"

Justin
Beaver

See? That's what I mean. Now tell me that's not funny! I don't just stick with the basic stuff. My humor is outside the box. "Now, *c'mon*, you know you *wanna* laugh. I'm like the Chris Rock of *Wiss-Miss*, (William Shatner Middle School — W.S.M.S. — We call it *Wiss-Miss*, which rhymes with Christmas, for short)," I said taking a bow.

"More like Chris Rock-Head," Grace fired back. *Ouch!* Then all the kids on line busted out laughing. Oh man, that's like a boxer landing a lucky punch. But I'm not worried, because I'm still the champ.

"Hey, Grace," I shouted loud enough for everyone to hear. "Careful when you're eating, you don't want your fork to hit against your metal teeth and cause a spark. You could burn down the school!" *Dag!* No laughs. If this was a cartoon you'd probably be hearing crickets now.

"Hey, I hear that instead of having a dentist appointment, your mom takes you to see a Blacksmith!" Nothing? *Ugh!* I'm dying here. See, this is the problem. I think that some of my jokes may be too clever for the kids at this school. I bet most of these *noobs** don't even know what a blacksmith is. They probably think it's one of my cousins whose last name is Smith. And from the looks of some of them, I'll bet they don't know what a dentist is either! *Man!* My parents could work the rest of their lives here and still not fix all the crooked teeth in this school!

"*C'mon*, man, this is 'A' material and none of you guys are laughing!"

"Well that's as close as you'll ever come to getting an 'A' in anything, Buck!" fired Grace again.

See, *now* they laugh at *her* stupid jokes, it's not even true either, my report card is full of A's. I make honor roll every semester! But do they laugh at *my* stuff? No! It's every comedian's nightmare. All right, I'm not going down without a fight.

"Hey, beaver," I started, "instead of standing on the lunch line, why don't you sit at a table … and eat *that?* The tables are wood, get it? That's what you beavers eat."

C'mon, now. If they're not laughing at *that*, then they have it in for me. I feel like I'm home with my three sisters. My *three-big-mouthed-evil-sisters*, I might add. Unfortunately, they don't think I'm funny either. Talk about a tough crowd. But when you grow up with *three-big-mouthed-evil-sisters*, then you really learn to take care of yourself. At least as far as insults.

*Check out the definition of *noobs* in the back of the book.

21

3 ½

MY THREE-BIG-MOUTHED-EVIL-SISTERS
— *by Buck Bievers*

I interrupt the story of my battle of wits with *brace-face-Grace*, who I'll also refer to as *Miss Justin Beaver*, to bring you a tale of an even greater battle with an even greater foe. Or in this case: *foes*. My sisters. Sorry, I mean my *three-big-mouthed-evil-sisters* Taylor, Trina and Tammy. They pick on me *all* the time, and for no reason, too. I think the only good thing they ever did was the time they braided my hair after they saw *The Karate Kid*. They said it would make me look like Jaden Smith. And they were *kinda* right. Some of the girls at school actually thought I *was* Jaden Smith. And I've been going to this school since *kindergarten!* Anyway, my sisters always seem to know the worst things to do to me. Like one time when they knew I pre-ordered a game for my Xbox three months ahead of time. Man, I counted down until the launch date every day. Only 56 days *'til* I get my game ... only 34 days left *'til* I get my game ... 12 days left *'til* I get my game ... Then the day it came out, I had my dad take me to pick it up before the line got too long. Sometimes those lines are ridiculous. I remember when that last C.O.D. (Call of Duty) came out, there *must've* been a hundred guys on line. Some of them even came dressed up like soldiers. Not sure if they were cool or *noobs*. See, when you're old enough to drive to GameStop by yourself, and you *still* come in costume, I think you're pushing it a bit. That's when the needle of your *cool-ometer* goes from the cool part into the crazy part. But that's just my opinion.

Anyway, my dad almost couldn't drive me because he had just taken my sisters — my *three-big-mouthed-evil-sisters* — to the Post Office to mail something and had to get back to work. So after I finally got my game, I raced home to play ... Only to find out that my *three-big-mouthed-evil-sisters* had just packed up all of my Xbox controllers and *mailed them to our house!* Now I know why they went to the Post Office ... *so they could mail my controllers!!! Ugh!!!*

That meant instead of playing my game the day I got it — the game that I had been waiting for months to play — the game that I had pre-ordered when I first heard about it — the game that I had watched every single trailer over and over again — Instead of playing *that* game, I had to wait three whole days until the mailman delivered my controllers back to my house! It wasn't even like they sent them Express Mail either!

They're just evil!

Now I know how Cinderella felt!

3 ¾

WHAT A DIS-GRACE

— by Buck Bievers

Okay where was I? I think I was talking about Grace "eating the table" or something which I *still* think is funny. I push my chest out proudly and look around to see if anyone else was laughing besides me. Sigh … the only one looking at me was Miss Mary, our head cook. Not exactly my target audience, but at least she's alive. At least, I *think* she's still alive. Rumor has it that she died 10 years ago, but they forgot to tell her so she still comes to work. It just goes to show what I was trying to tell you before, my jokes are for a more mature crowd. I just didn't think they had to be a hundred years old. I stare at Grace confidently and dare her to say something else.

"Jeez, Buck," she started. "Is it your jokes that stink, or did you just *cut the cheese* again?" Suddenly, milk came shooting out of Ezra's nose like a sprinkler watering his shirt. For a kid, that's the highest compliment a joke can get! Getting a "gusher" is like getting a gold medal in the Olympics. Dag, this is really *jacked up!* Here I am, the guy with the funniest sense of humor in the whole school, and I'm being taken down by a girl with fart jokes. This is really humiliating. It's like LeBron James being *taken to school* by some no-name rookie. This stinks. I mean it really stinks!

"And why can't you stand still like a normal person, Buck? You're always twitching and rocking back and forth like you have ants in your pants."

"Well obviously you guys don't really care about intelligent humor," I said, trying to shut her up so I could use the time to come up with some better jokes.

"Not that you have either intelligence *or* a sense of humor!" said Grace. Man, now she's really going for the kill!

Then I heard another voice. "Boy, why don't you just leave that poor girl alone? She wasn't bothering you. All she wanted was her lunch."

That voice belonged to Miss Mary, the head cook. Some folks say they call her the "head" cook 'cause she's in charge of our school's menu. But me? I think they call her that 'cause that's the secret ingredient in her Sloppy Joes. Heads! … *Human* heads!!! Don't believe me? Fine! All I know is that on *Sloppy Joe day*, I eat a salad!!! And it takes a lot for *me* to eat a salad.

I continued, "See, you guys just want to laugh at any stupid thing that comes to mind … Cooties! …" I yelled out while looking around. Finally some laughter. Nothing huge, just a few snickers. But at least it's a start.

"And don't get me started on the dumb lightning stripe that's shaved in your hair, who do you think you are, The Flash?"

Oh, no she didn't! I know she didn't just make fun of my lightning stripe! That's my trademark. Although I have to say that I am impressed that she knows who The Flash is. But still, she went too far! I took a piece of cake off the lunch counter.

"Here, Grace, have some cake, it's on me ... Actually, it's on YOU!"

I tossed it to her. See, the trick is that I didn't *throw* it. That might be seen as being violent, which would probably get me a date with the school psychologist. So I just tossed it at her to get a reaction. That way, if a teacher saw me do it, at least they knew I wasn't trying to hurt her.

But Grace, being the overly-dramatic princess that she is, really over-reacted. She flung her tray up in front of her face like she was trying to block a cannon ball or something. Her lunch spilled off her tray and down her shirt. It covered her whole front. It was great! Hey, maybe the school has security cameras and I could ask Principal Mushkin to burn me a DVD. Then I could post it on YouTube.

"Ha, you got *pwned,**" I said proudly.

What I didn't see was that when she flung her tray up to block the cake, the force launched her cup of strawberry yogurt into the air like a catapult. It flew clear across the room. Well, my jokes may not have hit their target today, but that yogurt sure did! It hit Principal Mushkin right in the center of his chest. The plastic cup stuck to him for a second like it was clinging to a loved one. Then slowly peeled off and plopped to the floor.

Splooch!

The yogurt, however, chose to hold on for dear life as it slowly began to slide down his tie all the way *'til* it reached his belt buckle. It looked like a fat lady in a pink bathing suit going down a water slide! Then it split into two separate pink streams that poured over his belt and began to run down the front of his pants like strawberry streams. If it wasn't for the fact that it was the principal, I swear this would be one of the funniest things I've ever seen in my whole life! Now if I can ever talk him into giving me *that* DVD, maybe I'll skip YouTube and send it straight to *America's Funniest Home Videos*. Man, I'll *betcha* I'd win first prize without a doubt. This is *wayyyy* funnier than someone hurting themselves on a trampoline or some kid trying to break open a piñata and hitting his dad in the *you-know-what*.

*Pronounced "poned." See the definition in the back of the book.

Although, I have to admit, that one always cracks me up. Hey, maybe he'd give me a copy if I promised to split the prize money with him.

You know the funny thing? He didn't even run to get a napkin like a normal person would do. Nope, he just stood there watching the little pink streams run down his pants like lava going down the side of a mountain. Yeah, I think I like that better than the waterslide description. That's called symbolism, we're studying it in English now. It was almost as if Mushkin didn't believe it was happening. Then he looked up to the ceiling and yelled out, "This is the worst day ever!"

A few kids snickered, but quickly bit their tongues to keep from getting in trouble.

"Who is responsible for this?" he demanded.

I can't tell if it was five kids, or 50 kids who said my name. But all I heard was, "BUCK!" I kept waiting for someone to say Grace's name. But no one ever did. I mean, not ONE person blamed her. In fact, the way they said my name, it sounded like a crowd of my fans chanting my name like I was on stage at a comedy club. Nope, there was no getting out of this mess.

"No fair," I said. "I'm a victim of racial profiling. I demand to see my lawyer."

"Thank you for the yogurt, Mr. Bievers," he said.

"No *problemo, my man*, would you like a drink, too?" I asked. Hey, if I was going down, the least I could do was go down in glory. I mean, it would be a shame to waste a good opportunity like that. After all, the crowd was already there. And you know what? They laughed. Every single one of them. Including Grace. I must've caused at least three milk gushers! Three! That was pure gold! "Thank you, thank you," I said while bowing to my adoring fans. "I'll be here all week."

"First of all, Mr. Bievers, I am *not* your *man*. Second, the only place you'll be all week ..." started the red-faced principal "... is in DETENTION!"

Dag! Now that's *not* funny. Not one bit.

4

FASHIONISTA
— *by Kimmy Kampbell*

My name is Kimmy Kampbell. That's Kampbell with a K, not a C. I *hate* when people spell it with a C, so the first step to being my friend is to remember that. Anyway, I'm the most popular girl in school, and I'm only in the sixth grade! I'm the tallest girl in my grade, too, like a supermodel, *and* I have the longest hair. My long red French braid goes all the way down my back. Just one more thing for all the skinny girls to be jealous of. That *plus* I have everything I want. And all the kids want what I have. Like all the absolute coolest designer clothes, the nicest boots, and the newest and most awesome electronics. I was the first one in the whole school to have an iPhone and an iPad. They're *so* cool! My daddy bought them for me the first day they came out. He lives in the city, so he always gets things first.

Now my mom, she used to be a model, so she knows everything there is about fashion. That's why all the kids in *Wiss-Miss* want to be just like me. Even the kids in the seventh and eighth grades, and they're in a whole *'nother* building. And if there's anyone who doesn't want to be like me, then it's because they're jealous. Whatever! It's like my mom always says, "People can be so petty sometimes."

But not me, I don't want to be like any of those *total fails*. Especially not those little skinny girls like Tessa and her *BFF* (more like her B-A-R-F) Samantha. Or as I call them, *Toothpick Tessa* and *Stringbing Samantha*. *OMG!* Speaking of the devil, or in this case, devils, here they come now. Watch! I'll bet the second they see me, *Toothpick* will lean over to whisper in *Stringbing's* ear. She'll probably be talking about how jealous she is of my new boots. They're Uggs, you know. The real ones, not the bootlegs that so many of the other kids around here wear.

"See something you like, *losers?*" I ask them, striking first.

"Well it's definitely not *you*," they say at the same time like the clones they are.

"Whatever! I'll bet you're just jealous of my new boots. Or is it my phone that you wish you had? It does everything. Plus I can even use it to Google *obnoxious skinny girls*, it would probably show me a photo of you!"

"Well I'm glad it's more than a phone," says Tessa "because I'm sure no one ever calls you, Kimmy! It's not like you've got any friends or anything."

"Yeah, Kimmy, and it's getting a little warm for boots, don't you think?" added Samantha.

See what I mean? Do you see how nasty people can be for no reason? It's amazing what jealously turns people into. All I can say is they're lucky my mom raised me to be a lady or I'd pound them even flatter than they already are. By the time I was done with them, they'd be flat as a sheet of notebook paper. Then I'd fold them up like a paper airplane, like on one of those cartoons, and fly them into the wind. That would be *so cool.*

"Well who needs friends? I've got a real *Prada* bag at home. I don't bring it to school, because I don't want any of you putting your greasy hands all over it." I make believe I'm typing with my fingers then I pretend to press a key with one finger as I yell, *"aaannnnddddd SEND!"* That's what I do when I deliver a really hot insult. I'll bet that hurt plenty.

"First of all, it's string BEAN! Not string BING," shrieked Tessa. "And have you ever stopped to think that I'm not the one with the weight problem? I'll bet even the Hulk would look skinny next to a moose like you, Kimmy!"

"Yeah, Kimmy. You're the one with the weight problem. You can't *wait* to eat!" chimed in Samantha as the two of them gave each other a high five while cackling like hyenas. "Maybe you wouldn't hate slim girls so much if you *were* one!"

"Yeah, Kimmy, and stop *dissin'* us in that stupid blog of yours! It's not like anyone reads it anyway!" said Tessa.

"OMG!" I said, "I'll bet that *Kimmy's Kolumn* is the most popular blog in the whole school. Maybe even the whole town. And you can bet that the only time you two get mentioned is when I do my weekly worst-dressed list!"

"You're wrong, Kimmy, you DID mention me in your stupid column. You wrote about my dad."

"Well I don't remember that."

"Well you did, Kimmy. And you got the story wrong, as usual!"

"I *never* get my stories wrong, *Stringbing.*"

"It's string *bean*, Kimmy!"

"Whatever!"

"And you *did* get it wrong. One night my dad was driving home late from work and he had to swerve off the road so he wouldn't hit a deer, but he hit a tree instead!"

"That's a lie, Samantha! I never wrote anything about your dad hitting a deer."

"I'm not done yet, Kimmy. He messed up the front of his car plus he could have gotten hurt. And when you overheard me tell Tessa that he had to get a new front bumper and headlights, you wrote about it."

"So? What's so bad about telling people your dad got headlights?"

"Well you wrote that my dad gave us all *head lice!!!*"

"Oh, yeah … *now* I remember. Well we had an outbreak, and my readers wanted to know where it came from. Besides, do you know for a fact that your father *doesn't* have head lice?"

"You're what they call a cyber-bully, Kimmy! I read about jerks like you in *Time for Kids*. You're just mean to everyone who's not fat like you! And who knows, you're probably mean to them, too!"

"I'm not a cyber-bully! Those are people who say mean things about kids and no one knows who they are. I sign my name to my work. And I'm not fat either!"

See, that's exactly what I mean. As soon as you try to be nice, they smell blood like a swarm of piranhas. So it's up to me to put a stop to this, and fast! I watched as they stood there laughing at me! I can't believe they called me fat. I'm not fat.

"My mother says that I'm just big-boned, that's all. She says I'll grow into my weight when I'm older, then I'll be just perfect."

"Well maybe if you grow to be 12 feet tall, Kimmy!"

"Yeah, Kimmy, then you'll look just like the She-Hulk! Only with red hair and not as pretty."

"See, I *knew* you were jealous of my hair. You wish you could put your hair in a French braid that could go all the way down your back. But you can't. It's the longest braid in the whole school. And you just wait, you'll be even more jealous when …" Then, the worst thing happened. I just stood there, still as a statue. My mind was blank. I couldn't think of anything else to say. No witty comeback. No cruel insult. Nothing. I can't believe it. They won. I can't believe they won.

Just then, Samantha opened the door to her locker, and a light bulb went on in my head. It was like a sign from above. "Hey, here's a riddle."

"Huh? A riddle?" they asked.

"How many *stringbings* can you fit into a locker?" I asked.

"I don't know," said Tessa.

"Yeah, how are we supposed to know? What kind of a stupid riddle is that? How many?"

"I don't know either," I said putting my books down. "But I'm about to find out!!!" Before they knew what hit them, I lunged forward and pushed Samantha towards her locker. She let out a short scream before I heard the small *thud* of some part of her body hitting the locker door. I kept pushing until she was all in. Then, in a flash, and before her evil twin realized what was happening, I reached out to grab ahold of her cheap sweater — acrylic I think — and pulled her towards me. Then I spun us both around and pushed her, too. I had to shove her even harder, because by now, Sam was trying to get out. Next I grabbed the door and swung it shut. One of them, and I don't know which, since now it was impossible to tell whose hands belonged to who (or is it *whom*), stuck out their skinny little arm to try to keep the door from closing. Too late! Whoever it was came about two seconds away from having to go through the rest of their life know as "lefty."

I shut the door. *SLAM!* And the sound of muffled screams filled the hallway. It was *so cool*. Who knows what they were babbling about, but I'm sure it was a cross between, "Let us out," and calling me names. She-Hulk! *Humph!* But not once in all of that yelling and carrying on did I ever hear anything that even remotely sounded like, "I'm sorry, Kimmy," or, "Please forgive us, Kimmy." If I had any regrets about stuffing them into this locker, that feeling didn't last for more than a second or two. See, when mean kids force me to do stuff like this, I usually don't have any regrets. In fact, the only time I've ever regretted something like this was when I got Robby for hitting me with a snowball by making a 20-foot Robby-angel.

Know how to make one of those?

Well, it's pretty simple. First I pushed him into the snow. Then, before he could get up, I grabbed his legs and began pulling him from one end of the playground to the other. And since he was flapping his arms like a turkey the whole time, it came out looking like a snow angel. A really tall snow angel! *OMG*, it was *so cool!*

The only problem was that I didn't find out until later that it was actually Cameron who hit me with the snowball. Not Robby. Oh, well. You

win some and you lose some. Even though I guess I really didn't lose.

After all, I'M not the one who got dragged in the snow.

The sounds of the pipsqueaks' little skinny fists banging on the inside of the locker door brought me out of my daydream. Should I let them out? Or should I walk away and leave them? I could also threaten to pound anyone who was bold enough to let them out. Yeah, I could do that. I'll walk off and leave them to think about taking responsibility for their actions. This would also make a really good entry for my blog. Maybe even on Twitter. Yes, I do believe I'll *Tweet* it.

As I turned to leave, all the lights went out. And there was something on my face, *kinda* wet, and it smelled like strawberries. Not real strawberries, but like something artificially flavored. Yuck, this is weird. When I took a step back, I realized the lights weren't out after all. I had just walked face first into Principal Marshmallow. *Ewww*, his shirt was wet. Well, I'm glad he's here, because now I can tell him what those two pancakes did to me and get them in even more trouble.

He looked at me, then looked at the row of lockers to see where the noise was coming from. I couldn't wait for him to punish that *dorky duo*, so I pointed to the locker. "They're in there," I said proudly.

He followed the direction of my finger and lifted the handle of the door. The two girls poured out of the locker like my fish poured out of my fish tank when I was little and I accidentally broke the glass while playing a Mario game on my WII. *Thud!*

Right on the floor they went. The girls, not my fish. The fish made more of a *sploosh* sound. Not to worry, my dad bought me an even bigger fish tank filled with bigger fish the very next day. He just didn't put it near the WII. You should have seen the way the girls fell out of the locker. It was *so cool!* They sat up on their knees and immediately started shouting like two crazy girls.

"It was Kimmy, she shoved us into the locker and shut the door!"

"Yes, I know," said the Principal, "I witnessed the entire incident, including the name calling."

Perfect! I know someone who's about to get a …

"Detention!" he said.

"Hah!" I laughed in their direction. *"aaannnnddddd SEND!"*

The weird part was that they started laughing, too. Boy, those girls are even stranger than I thought! I looked up at Principal Marshmallow in order to see him glaring at the girls. But he wasn't looking at them. He was looking at *me!* Why in the world would he be looking at me?

"Detention, Miss Kampbell," he said.

"Miss Kampbell? But that's my name! No, Samantha's last name is… wait a minute … m-m-e-e-e?" I asked stuttering. What was going on here? "But it was them, they started it!" I said, defending myself.

But he just kept looking at me. "Why do *I* get detention? They were the ones who started it. I was just minding my own business when they started calling me fat! That's how it happened. I'M the victim, not *them!* Why are you punishing *me*?!"

From then on, I didn't hear much of anything. It was like on one of those old Charlie Brown cartoons that come on during the holidays where you hear that funny sound whenever the grown-ups talk. *Whah whah whah…* All I know is that I could see everyone laughing. And they were laughing at *me*. This is the second time today I've been laughed at. I don't know how some of these nerdy kids cope with that, but I know I don't like it. Not one bit!

"You're all jealous of me, all of you! You wish *you* had the new iPhone, it's 6G!!! Maybe even 7G!!!" I screamed. Then I felt the principal's hand on my shoulder guiding me away from the laughing kids. He was really sending me to detention. *Me*, of all people!!!

"And I'm going to get an even newer phone, too. It's going to be 8G!"

I picked up my books and headed in the direction of the school's version of jail. "Whatever!" I said as I stomped down the hallway.

"And we need to talk about that blog of yours, too!" said Principal Marshmallow. "I think I have rather nice taste in ties!"

This is definitely *not cool!*

Over 3.2 million students are victims of bullying each year.
— DoSomething.org

5

WHO'S A JOIK?!

— *by Bobby Bonderman*

"C'mon, *Weggie*, say it! Say it!!!"

Of all the kids to pick on, I *gotta* say that Reggie Roberts is my very favorite. He's not like some kids who only have one or two things to pick on. He's got so many issues, it's hard to figure out which one to choose. He's like an all-you-can-eat buffet. To begin with, he's a real porker. He looks like he's never met a dessert he didn't like. He's bigger than most sixth graders, and even a few seventh graders, and he's only in the *fifth* grade. Man, if I was his size (just the tall part, not the fat part.) I'd be running things at this stupid school! I'd even boss around the eighth graders. Man, that would be awesome. And you know what's really funny? Whenever I send Reggie home whining, he *never* tells on me. Ever! So I can probably keep this up 'til we're grown-ups and never get in trouble.

And you know what his mom does to stop him from *bawlin'* like a big baby? She gives him ice cream. Ice cream! I'm not talking about just one scoop like we get at my house, either. My mom acts like she's giving away a kidney the way she dishes out those tiny portions. Reggie gets at least *three huge scoops!* I heard him tell someone. Plus a few cherries, and even that chocolate topping that gets real hard and crunchy. My mom doesn't like us to eat a lot of sweets! That's why my step-brother Bryce keeps a stash of junk food in the back of his closet. He thinks no one knows about it, but I do. Anyway, the sadder *Weggie* gets, the more he eats. Then the more he eats, the bigger he gets. And the bigger he gets, the more fun I can have with him. It's like the more I pick on him, the easier he makes it for me! Man, I hope life is always this easy. I put down my soccer ball and put Reggie in my patented hammer grip.

"I'm warning you, *Weggie*, you'd better say it soon, or you're *gonna* get a sandwich. And I don't mean the kind you want either. No mayonnaise, just my knuckles."

You know the other thing that makes him my favorite target? He's really weak, too. Don't ask me how I can be stronger than a kid who's almost twice my size … but I am. *Lots!* I can't tell if he's really just a weakling, or if he's just too afraid to fight back. And his dad obviously hasn't taught him *anything* about how to stand up for himself. That's 'cause he's always working. Reggie's dad works even more than my dad! No one ever sees the guy. Even at parents day, it's always only his mom who shows up. But I'll bet his dad is a *wimp,* too. Probably still gets his lunch money taken from him at his office.

All I know is that it makes me look really cool for someone my size to be able to rough up someone his size. I mean, not that I'm tiny or anything. Well at least I *ain't* the smallest kid in my class. Parker is. And there are a few girls, too. But we're not talking about me, my mom says that I'm just a late bloomer. By the time I'm in high school, I bet I'll be six feet tall!

But enough about me. Let me tell you about Weggie's pants! They're not only tight, and almost always plaid, but they're usually about three inches too short. They're almost my size. Another inch higher and they could pass for shorts. His poor ankles must freeze in the winter! And you can always see the bottom of his big belly sticking out from under his shirt. Gross! Anyway, I think the thing I like next about Reggie is that he talks funny. Doesn't even say his own name right. Can't say the letter "R" to save his life. He made me laugh so hard one day I almost puked. So I try not to pick on him right after lunch anymore. Watch and I'll show you what I mean. But don't get mad at me if you puke on your shirt.

"Last chance, dude!"

"Okay, okay, I'll say it! M--m--my name is W-Weggie."

"Huh? Can't hear ya. Say it again. And louder this time!" See this part is called playing the crowd.

"*Ow!* Bobby stop it! Why won't you *weave me a-wone?*" pleaded Reggie.

"Just say it! And I might let you go!" I shot back.

"W-W-Weggie!"

Ahhh, music to my ears. "Well if you insist, one wedgie coming up!"

"No, I didn't say wedgie, I said Weggie. R-E-G-G-I-E! You're just making fun of the way I *tawk!*" replied Reggie as his voice began to soften and crack.

"Sorry, can't hear ya, dude, too busy giving you the wedgie you asked for!" Man, this is awesome! Now all I *gotta* do is grip the back of his underwear and p-u-llllllllllllllllllllll!

"Ow!" shrieked Reggie.

"You don't like me do you, Bryce?" I asked.

"*Bwyce*? Why did you call me *Bwyce*?" asks Reggie.

"Bryce?! Nobody said anything about Bryce!"

"Uh-huh, you just did!"

"Listen, Weggie, I *know* what I said."

I already know the answer. But I don't need him to like me anyway. But you know what, in some bizarre way, he just might like me *'cause* this is probably the only attention he gets here at school. Maybe at home, too. Yeah, if it wasn't for me, no one would even know he existed. He'd be one of the kids who when you look at your school yearbook in twenty years, you'd be like "hmmm, where did this fat kid come from? He must have just transferred that year."

"So do you like me or not, *Weggie?*" I asked again.

"N-n-not *weal-wy,*" whimpered Reggie. "You're ch …"

"Chinese?! Dude, what are you some *kinda* racist?"

"I never said Chinese. Besides, I thought you were *Ko-wean!*"

"I *am* Korean. So if you already knew, why did you call me Chinese?!"

"I didn't call you Chinese. But even if you were, it wouldn't matter. I don't *wike* you because you're childish. And you're a … a … a …"

"Adopted?" I asked. "That's really low, dude! I'm not the only adopted kid in this school. So you're telling me that the reason you hate me is *'cause* I'm Korean and I'm adopted?"

"No, you're a *joik!!!*"

"A jerk?!! Oh, well at least you're not a racist." Boy *ol' Weggie* might be getting some backbone after all. The crowd of kids gathered around us got even bigger. No laughter yet, so I need to step up my game.

"Okay, Obi-Wan, time to come out!" I said as I tugged on the elastic waistband of his Star Wars underwear a second time. But I apparently tugged too hard and made Reggie lose his balance. He began to fall. And there was nothing I could do to stop him. It was like it was all in slow motion. I panicked, and as I moved, he moved, too. But when I tried to back away, I stepped on my stupid soccer ball. I fell. And he fell, too. Right on top of me! It was like a scene from an *Itchy and Scratchy* cartoon when a piano or something heavy falls on top of someone. The next thing I felt was all of the air being forced out of my lungs. I thought my eyes were going to pop out of my head and start bouncing around the hallways like ping pong balls.

Sure, *now* people laugh. And laugh … And laugh …

Then that sound of cackling was broken by a man's voice.

"Mr. Bonderman!"

Oh crap, it's Principal Marshman, or as I like to call him sometimes, Principal *Martian!* I call him that because he acts like he's from another planet or something. I hope he didn't see the whole thing or else I'm in trouble. Man, I *gotta* get me a look-out to warn me when this guy's coming. Slowly I open my eyes to see a glowing light saber right in front of my eyes. *E-y-ewww!* That means Weggie's butt is right in front of my face and all I can see is his underwear!

"What are you doing to that boy?" our alien principal asked.

I try to speak, but there's still no air in my lungs. And Reggie is still sprawled out on top of me. All I can do is let out a gasp. Finally he leaned over and helped Reggie up. I have never been so happy to breathe in my life. My lungs felt like two deflated basketballs finally getting pumped up again. I laid there for a few minutes.

"What were you doing to Reggie?" he asked again.

Okay, Bobby think fast. "I'm uh … uh … helping him." I pause a second to take another breath, and to give me a chance to come up with a good story. "See, I was just walking by minding my own business, when I saw poor Weggie … I mean Reggie here. It looks like his underwear got stuck on his locker door. So I stopped to try to help get him free. And when I tugged, he lost his balance and fell. I tried to catch him, but you see how fat … uh … I mean, how much bigger he is than me. These guys all saw it, just ask them."

"Mr. Bonderman! There's no need to ask anyone, I know what I see. I see a boy with a need for power who is using his strength to pick on a kid who is different. Yes, he's different, Mr. Bonderman. And so are you."

"*Me?!*" I asked.

"And so am I," he added. "And that's exactly what makes this planet a wonderful place to live. Can you imagine if we were all exactly the same? Wouldn't that be boring? What if everyone looked exactly like you, Bobby, what would the world look like?"

"Like Munchin-land from the *The Wizard of Oz*," yelled a voice from the crowd.

"Or maybe that movie with the *oompa loompas! Willie Wonka!*"

"Who said that?!" I snapped. If I ever find out, I'll give him something to be sorry for. Unless it's that freaky Mexican kid Dex! If it's him, I'll just pretend I didn't hear it. He's the only kid in the whole school who scares me.

"And you!" said Principal Martian looking at all of the kids who were watching. "I can't believe you all stood there watching him pick on this innocent boy. In my book, that makes you just as guilty. Those of you who stood by and did nothing are just as guilty as Bobby! If you're afraid to speak up to him, then it's your duty to go get a teacher. If it was you being picked on, wouldn't you want someone to help?"

No answer from the crowd. Most of them just looked down at their feet.

"Well, wouldn't you?"

"Yes," they all said *sheepishly*. That was one of my vocab words earlier this year. It means shy or timid. You know, like sheep.

"Now as far as you, *Mr. Bonderman*. I need you to take much more responsibility for your actions. I need you to admit that what you've done is wrong. What I don't want to hear are any excuses. Just two words, 'I'm sorry.' That's all I want from you."

"Well I DO have two words," I said, "I'm innocent!"

"In that case, I have two more for you, as well!" said our funny-looking principal.

"Dentenion ... now!"

Shoot! I hate detention. I'd rather eat my mom's *kimchi**, and I hate my mom's *kimchi!!!* I'll tell you more about that later.

"Yes, sir," I said while shooting Reggie one last dirty look. I'll get him back later for getting me in trouble.

*See Bobby's guide in the back of the book

6
DETENTION TO DETAIL
— *by Buck Bievers*

"Preeeeeeeeeeeeeeeeeeeeeeeesenting the star of stage and screen, please welcome Buuuuuuuck Bie-verrrrrrrrrrs," I said as I opened the door to detention. Hey, if I *gotta* be stuck in this joint for an hour, then I'm *gonna* make it fun. They may lock up my body, but they will *never* lock up my mind. "Thank you, thank you, I'll be here all week. Wish it wasn't so, but it is."

But the room was empty. Guess I'm the first one here. Oh well, that means I get to pick my seat. (Well it beats picking my nose.) Right in the middle, my favorite place to be. Wonder who else is on the guest list?

I sit and take out my notebook and start drawing and writing some jokes. I *gotta* think of some good stuff for Grace. Man, I can't believe no one laughed at "brace face." Let's see, something with teeth … beaver, no too much like my last name, don't want kids to start calling *me* that. Tooth Fairy, Timmy Turner, the-whole-tooth-and-nothing-but-the-tooth … I tear out a sheet of paper and begin to fold it. Not making anything in particular, just giving my hands something to do *'til* I come up with some jokes.

It's three o'clock and all the kids in school are laughing as they walk to the circle on their way to catch the bus or to practice for their teams. What I wouldn't give to be out there with them, instead of having to spend the next hour sitting here in detention. Not only is this a waste of time, but this is one of the worst classrooms in the whole school. For one thing, it's always dark. Don't know why that is, even with the lights on, this room always just looks dim. And it smells funny, too. It's right near the garbage bin that's behind the cafeteria, so there's always some *kinda* funky smell in the air. Man, you should get a whiff of it when the weather is hot and it's full of leftover meatloaf. *Whew!* It's like spending the day at the dump!

After a few minutes, the door opens and a girl walks in. Oh great! It's that crazy girl who is obsessed with playing four-square! The one who always plays barefoot. She's the same maniac who gave that *dude* Nick a black eye. Or maybe it was a bloody nose. Then while all the kids ran over to see if he was okay, she stood there smiling an insane-kinda-smile. Man! She even freaked *me* out.

She sits up in the front of the class like she always does so she can be near the teacher. Craving attention. I think it's because kids don't like her so she feels more comfortable around adults. Yeah, adults and other creepy things like spiders, scorpions, piranha fish … She reaches into her pocket and pulls something out. It's probably a snack like raw meat or live worms that she'll slurp down one at a time like strands of spaghetti. *Hmmm*, nope, not raw meat. It was a balled-up tissue that she peeled open like she was unwrapping a Christmas present. Then she took out what looked like a necklace, looked at it for a few minutes, then put it around her neck. There was something that hung from it, which knowing her is probably a skull and crossbones or some other symbol of evil to match that freaky black ring that she always wears. But I can't see it from here. After that she just *kinda* sat there for a while, either playing with the red feather in her hair or twisting her evil black ring around her finger.

Speaking of evil. When the door opened again my other "favorite person in the whole wide world" stepped in. And I'm saying that with as much sarcasm as I can pack into one sentence. I think her name is Kimmy something. She's a big girl. Not necessarily fat, but solid. Like a wrestler. Man, I'll bet she'd give anyone a run for their money in a hot-dog-eating contest. And she's got that super long red braid that she keeps in the front so it almost touches her belly button. It's like a red tail or something. She also sits in the front row, close to the door, so she's the first one you'll notice when you walk in. She's another mean one, but I'm not exactly sure which one of them is the worst. She might be a little weirder since she's still wearing her winter boots even though it's spring. Then she looks over at crazy girl and slides her chair up another foot so there's no doubt as to who's in the front.

Man! Girls are weird.

Then *Psycho-Four-Square-Girl* slides up to be even more in front. Looks like they're about to have a chair race or something. That'd be *kinda* funny. After Kimmy slides up another inch and shoots *Psycho* a look, she reaches in her bag, takes out a mirror and starts checking herself out. Then she starts stroking her red braid like she's stroking her pet tarantula. I'll bet the best part about being that in love with yourself is that you're always with someone who loves you back just as much.

Now just when I thought it was only going to be the three of us, the door opened again and that kid Dex walks in. *Ugh!* At least the girls will probably talk, this kid never says *nothing*. I guess he's just too cool for words. Or maybe he just doesn't speak any English. Maybe all he knows is Mexican. All he ever does is sit in the back of the class leaning back in his chair like he's posing for the cover of *Moody Middle Schoolers' Magazine*. He's like a kid from a movie about one of those schools full of grumpy kids that gets a new principal or teacher or someone who wants to prove that they can teach even the worst kids how to read. Then by the end of the movie they're all quoting Shakespeare.

But Dex is definitely the *before* version, not the *after*. I don't think he'll ever be the *after*. He's got on his trademark red sweatshirt with the neck zipped all the way up. *C'mon,* people, it's not that cold out anymore!!! Plus he's got his other trademark. His *shades,* which are always either on his face, or up on top of his head. Dex headed straight to the back of the classroom and took the seat closest to the window. I'll bet he's here so much that they reserve that desk just for him. Man, if they wanted to punish me, they sure picked the right kids to lock me up with. I'd be happier if they just pushed me into a pit full of snakes. At least I might have a chance of finding one with a personality. I wish someone else would come. Someone who I could actually talk to. Anyone!

My mom always says to be careful what you wish for. I never fully understood it until now. Because when the door opened again, in walked *Mr. Wedgie* himself. Bobby Bonderman! In history, we learned about this dude named Napolean, he was a French general or something way back in, *like,* the late 1700s and early 1800s. This guy was ruthless. Just like Bobby. Wanted to rule the world, just like Bobby. Anyway, he was supposed to be a real little dude. Like maybe two feet tall or something. Also just like Bobby. And it was because he was so small that he wanted to show how tough he was. Overcondensation ... No wait, com ... pen ... Overcompensation! That's it! That's where they get the term "Napolean complex" from. It means a short guy who tries to make up for his lack of height by doing all kinds of stuff to show how tough he is. And Bobby is just like that. A tiny little Chinese kid who tries to show how tough he is by beating up on wimpy fat kids. In fact, he'd make a great villain in the *Diary of a Wimpy Kid* books. He really *is* a jerk! He comes in kicking his stupid soccer ball that he always has with him, then takes a seat.

I unfold the piece of paper and begin to rip it into long narrow strips. Well this room may be a lot of bad things, but at least it's diverse. It's already got the Black kid (me), the Asian kid, the Hispanic kid, whatever *Psycho-Four-Square-Girl* is and even a white kid. This would be a great photo for the diversity newsletter. William Shatner Middle School: where kids of all races come to get in trouble. Or how about, "At W.S.M.S., the letter 'D' isn't just for detention, it's also for diversity!" I can't wait to see who comes in next! The Indian kid in seventh grade? The girl with two moms? The kid in fifth grade who no one knows what he is? … No, those guys never get in any trouble. But even a pack of rabid wolves would be an improvement from this group. At least then, my suffering would be over quickly, as opposed to this slow painful death that I'm about to suffer over the next hour. I can't say I don't belong here, but I'm not like these guys. I'm funny! *They're* just plain mean. There's a big difference. I like to make people laugh. They like to make people cry! It's not my fault people don't get my jokes.

The uncomfortable silence seemed to last forever, but it was probably actually only about a few minutes. Too much quiet makes me nervous. Probably because from the time I was born, my house has never been quiet for a single second. And if you've got sisters, you know exactly what I mean. There's always someone on the phone, or blasting a CD, watching something on YouTube or arguing over whose turn it is to use the bathroom. So it's not my fault that I can't stand to be in a room full of people and not have anyone talking. That's my downfall. Got me labeled the class clown, but it's just tough to be quiet for that long. But if the girls can be quiet, I guess I can, too!

I grab my pen and pretend like it's a microphone. "Good evening, ladies and jelly beans, welcome to detention. I'm your host Buck Bievers. So, what's your name, what are you in for?" Okay, so maybe I can't stay quiet.

Nothing. Not a sound. *Dag!* This is just not my day.

"Let's see a show of hands, how many of you are in for murder? Anyone? Just me? … Well all righty then. … Arson? … No? Only me for that, too, huh? No pyromaniacs? Good, I hate pyromaniacs. You think they're you're friends, but you always end up getting *burned*. Get it? Google pyromanics, you'll get it then. Anyone for assault? … A-pepper? How *'bout* you *Four-Square-Girl*? What's your name and who'd you beat down this time?"

"My name is Mina, and I'm going to, *like,* beat *you* down if you don't shut up."

"And I'll help her," added the chunky girl.

"Great, at least everyone's talking now. How *'bout* you Fonzie, what are you in for?" I asked Dex. Ever see Fonzie from *Happy Days*? It was a TV show from back when my folks were kids, I watch the reruns.

Dex just turned and looked out the window.

"Oh, sorry, let's try this: ¿Como estas, amigo?"

He turned and glared at me. Uh-oh. Then he looked away. Good, *'cause* that look actually scared me for a minute. I continued, "I don't know about you, but I sense a connection here. I think this detention is going to bring us all closer together. Hey, maybe my mom can call your mom and schedule a playdate when this is all over. Are we too old for playdates? I think we're supposed to call them 'hang-outs' now. Maybe you guys can come over to my house and not talk to me there, too. Hey, how *'bout* you Tiny Tim? What did you do, give the principal one of your patented wedgies? Or did you punch him in the kneecap?"

"No he didn't," interrupted Principal Mushkin.

Dag! It's like that guy just appears *outta* thin air or something. No, really. You can never hear him sneaking up on you. Never! He freaks me out.

"I've brought you all here today because you have all done something that has gotten you in trouble," he started. "There are no innocent victims in this room. And unfortunately, this isn't the first time for any of you. As your principal, I find no joy in sending anyone to detention. But I can not have anyone in this school feel like they're above the rules. Or that they are better than anyone else. You are all guilty of both."

"But what if you really *are* better than other kids?" asked an insulted Kimmy. "This blouse is *Dolce & Gabbana!* And I had the first iPhone in the entire school. Including teachers."

"Miss Kampbell, what you fail to realize is that material possessions do not make people special. People make themselves special by their actions. Kindness. Love. Respect. The effort you give. That's what makes you special. Not an iPhone."

"But it's got a built-in GPS!" said Kimmy.

Okay, I think if I had to choose, she might even be more psycho than *Psycho-Four-Square-Girl.* I don't normally insult people who can beat me up, or sit on me, but in this case I was about to make an exception.

"GPS? What in the world do you need a GPS for?" I asked "To find your way to the cafeteria three times a day?"

The other three detainees busted out laughing. Finally! An audience that can appreciate a good joke. Then I imitated her voice, "Look at my underwear, they're *Dull-chay and Banana*, too!" More laughter. Jackpot! Even the Mexican kid cracked up.

"Mr. Bievers, quiet! … Miss Kampbell, you come to school to learn. School is not a punishment, it is your duty! Not only are you here to learn subjects like math and science that will help you when you get older, but it's part of your social development. It helps you learn how to get along with other kids your age. In class, clubs, sports teams … And in the cases where you can't get along, you learn how to resolve conflict. When your teachers give you a test, it's not to embarrass you. Tests are designed to show us how much you understand. If you do well, then we know that we have taught you properly."

Oh, man, this guy is boring. This is the longest speech ever.

Unfortunately he didn't stop there. "But if you do poorly, we know that we need to give you more help. Now if *everyone* does poorly, then we know we must change how we teach, because obviously it's not working. So when you cheat, or have someone do your homework for you (he glared at Dex), you're not just cheating your classmates and your teachers, but you are really cheating yourselves, too. Which is worse because when you do that, it's your way of admitting that it's always better to take the easy way out. You're saying that instead of preparing by studying, you'd rather cheat."

Dex sighed out loud and turned his head to look out the window again. That must be what he got busted for. Either cheating on a test or having some brainy kid do his homework for him. I never looked at it that way before, but I guess what the principal is saying is right. I guess it does mess it up for everyone.

"And as for you, Mr. Bonderman. Have you ever thought what it would be like to trade places with Reggie? What would you need in order to be him?"

"Bigger clothes?" he said.

Omigosh, that was genius. Why can't anyone ever set me up with straight lines like that? It was too easy. Needless to say, we all laughed for about the next ten minutes.

"Another comment like that, Mr. Bonderman, and you will spend the rest of the semester in this room!"

"Sorry, sir."

"As I was saying, have you ever imagined how tough it might be for kids like Reggie to even come to a place everyday knowing he'll be teased because of his weight? Or what if you have braces? Or you're not as good an athlete as other kids? You even tease kids for being too smart! How can you tease someone for being smart?! You kids treat it like a handicap. That's how backwards your society is. You reward laziness and cruelty. I've never seen anything like it."

Bobby stood up to defend himself, "Yeah, but I wasn't really trying to —"

"It's not always your *intent*, it's the *impact* of your actions. And let's be honest, how can you pull on someone's underwear in front of all of his classmates and think that anything good could ever come of it?"

Wow, he sure shut Bobby up. In fact, he shut us all up. We couldn't wait for him to stop, but unfortunately, he wasn't done yet.

"If I constantly scream at you, but don't mean to hurt your feelings, does that make it hurt less?" Then he looked at Kimmy and started again. "Kimmy, if I pick up this book and throw it at your head, would it hurt?" he asked.

"Sure, it would hurt a lot," answered Kimmy.

He continued, "Now what if I picked up the book and tried to throw it out the window, instead? But it still hits you in the head. Would that make a difference?"

"Duh! I'm still being hit in the head with a book! Of course it will hurt!"

"So, the *impact* is not determined by the *intent*?"

"Uh, I'm more of a visual guy," I said "could you actually throw the book at her to help me understand?" You should have seen the look that Kimmy shot me. I decided to give a serious answer before she got too mad. "Well, she might forgive you if it's an accident, but it would still hurt the same."

"So if you make fun of someone because they have braces, and everyone laughs, does it hurt less just because you were joking?" he said looking at me. Man, I *shoulda* kept my mouth shut!

You all have to learn to understand that this is how it starts, when you're young. Kids who cheat become adults who cheat. That's why the jails are full. People do *not* take responsibility for their actions. They don't put in the effort to learn to read or write, so their options are limited. Even the sports you play shouldn't be as much about winning as much as they should be about teamwork."

"Yeah, especially our teams. They never win!" I said. Not a huge laugh. More nervous laughter than anything. I think we were all starting to feel bad. But I was trying anything to stop this guy from talking. I don't know about the other kids, but he's making *me* feel awful. "Thank you, thank you, I'll be here all week," I added.

"Actually, you *will* be here all week, Mr. Bievers! You all will," said the Principal.

"What? All week?!" we screamed at the same time.

"Yes, I don't think that an hour is a fitting punishment for the crimes that you've all committed since you've been in this school. We're not talking about one-time offenses. You're being punished for your behavior over a period of time."

Crimes? Who is he, Judge Judy? *Dag!* This really stinks.

I take out my notebook and start to draw. I can do a pretty good *Goku* from *Dragon Ball Z*.

"And if I have to send you all to detention every single day for the rest of the year to show you that it's not okay to be a cheat, or be a bully, or post mean things about kids on the Internet, then I will. Because bullies aren't just kids who pick on other kids physically, there is also mental bullying such as insults, put downs, racism, classism, cyber-bullying …"

Wait a minute, he can't group me in with these guys, "But it's not our fault, maybe those *noobs* just can't take a joke!" I said.

The Principal continued … again, "Mr. Bievers, it's one thing if you joke around with your peers or your friends —"

"Buck doesn't have friends," said someone, I'm not sure who, since I was too busy freaking out from this never-ending speech.

"I don't have a problem with that, Buck. Or even if you joke with the other kids in this room, since you all can dish it out. But if you're someone who enjoys teasing kids who don't like it, and can't defend themselves, then in my book that makes you a bully! If I could, every kid who watched what you did and didn't tell a teacher would be in here as well. It's bullies like you who make up terms like *snitching* or *tattle tale*. That's how you convince other kids not to do the right thing and turn you in. You kids don't know what it's like to not fit in … and … and … if you do, then you really shouldn't make … other kids feel … that … way … *ugh* …"

"Not fit in? You think I don't know what it feels like *not* to fit in?" asked Bobby. "Try being Korean and adopted in this school. It's not like there are a lot of us here. Or having a big brother who … who … nevermind. And as far as me not being punished enough, you're making me miss soccer practice. That's punishment."

"Well try being Puerto Rican!" yelled Fonzie.

"You're Puerto Rican?" asked Psycho-Four-Square-Girl. "I always thought you were Mexican!"

"See?" he said. "That's what I mean. Nobody here ever cares enough to remember that I'm not Mexican, I'm Puerto Rican! *No me importa**!" He turned and looked out the window again.

"Well if that's how you feel … " said the principal, who all of a sudden was talking very slowly, almost like he was in pain, "… why go out of your way to make others feel bad as well? Does making another kid feel bad make you feel better? … *ugh!*" He stopped again and wiped his forehead with a tissue. Boy, he's really starting to sweat.

"And by the way, my name is Principal *Marshand!* It is not Mushkin, not Marshkin, not Marshman, Milkman or Marshmallow. M-A-R-S-H-A-N-D! Marshand!" he said glaring at all of us.

Then, right in the middle of his sentence he started to stutter. And sweat some more. It was like all of a sudden he just got weak or something because he needed to prop himself up on the desk. I warned him not to eat Miss Mary's fish tacos. I think her special sauce is mercury. The catch of the day is botulism (which I think is some kind of food poisoning. Google that, too).

"What time is it?" he yelled out. "I asked you the time!"

"3:15,"said Kimmy looking at her iPhone or iWatch or whatever new gadget she was holding.

"*Ugh!* … I got so caught up dealing with you … you … bullies, that I forgot …" he said heading to the door.

"Forgot what?" asked Mina.

But he didn't stop. He went through the door and ran stumbling down the hallway.

We all stared at the door as it slammed shut behind him. After a minute or two, we turned and stared at each other.

"*Ummm* ... so what do we do now, dudes?" asked Bobby.

"*Shoot*, if he *ain't* here, I'm going home. How will he know?" said Dex.

"Maybe I can still catch some of soccer practice," added Bobby.

"No, we need to see if he's okay. Don't we?" That was my question to the group. But no one seemed to want to answer. "C'mon, let's go ... maybe he's really sick."

No response. Even more quiet than if I had told one of my jokes. You know, if I didn't know better, I'd swear I had lost my voice or something. It's like people haven't heard a word I've said all day.

"Well I'm going, you can come with me or you can stay here and rot in detention," I said. I ran out the class to see if I could catch up with Mushkin. I mean Marshand. As slow as he was stumbling around, it shouldn't be too hard. After a few steps, I heard the door to detention swing open. I guess some of the guys decided to join in after all. I bet it's the boys: Fonzie and Napoleon. But when I turned around, it was all four of them.

"Kimmy? Psycho-Four-Square-Girl? You're actually coming to see if someone is okay?" I asked surprised?

"Well anything is better than staying in that dark, stinky room," said Kimmy.

"Yeah, it smells like feet! And by the way, my name is Mina, not Psycho-Four-Square-Girl!"

Uh-oh, did I really just call her that out loud? *Oops, my bad.*

"I heard a sound from down there, *bro*," said Fonzie.

"Wow, your English is pretty good," I said while giving him the thumbs up sign. "Muy bien!"

But instead of saying, "mucho gracias," or something, he just rolled his eyes. What?! I just gave him a compliment! We turned down the hallway only to see a whole section of the wall closing like a giant door. It's the wall right behind that life-sized *knight in shining armor* that's in between two rows of lockers. Even though it's not really shiny. To tell you the truth, it's pretty dingy and dusty. But as we got closer, it looked like there was a hallway behind the wall, like out of one of those creepy horror movies. Fonzie slid a recycle bin across the floor to keep the door from closing all the way. It worked.

"I'm going in," he said.

Man! I really wish he hadn't!

6 1/2
AND HERE'S WHERE MY LIFE GETS WEIRD
— *by Buck Bievers*

"I'm going in!" said Dex again, "who else is *down?*"

Down is cool talk for who else is going to do it. But you probably know that already. I'll bet Dex never says anything that's not cool. He could even find a way to say, "I have to *pee pee,*" and make it cool. Something like, *"Yo, bro, I gots ta take the P-train, knowhudumsayin'?"* And of course, I'd have no idea what he was saying.

Next thing I know, the five of us are slowly creeping down a dark staircase as the secret door closes behind us. When we hear the slam we all turn and look at Bobby who was the last in line.

"What?!" he said.

"Why didn't you prop the door open so we can get back out? Now we might be trapped down here."

"Prop it open with what?" he asked.

"With the recycle bin! You could have even used your stupid soccer ball!" said Mina.

"No way!" he said. "My ball goes where I go."

We continued down the dark stairs. It was like a scene out of a *Scooby Doo Mystery.* Hey, as long as I'm Fred, I don't mind. I definitely don't want to be Shaggy. Although, he *is* the funniest. Okay, so maybe I'll be Shaggy after all; Fonzie will be Fred; Kimmy is Daphne; and Mina is Velma. Guess that means that Bobby is Scooby. Actually, maybe I should call him *Booooby* so it rhymes with *Scooby.* Yeah, that's even better. Then imitating Scooby Doo's voice I yelled out, *"Booooby Booooooooooo."* You know, I really didn't mean to say that out loud. In fact, I didn't realize that I had even done it *'til* they all stopped and stared at me. I guess I do that occasionally.

"Um, do you need, *like*, meds or something?" Psycho-Four-Square-Girl, I mean Mina, asked me.

Actually, now that she mentions it, I did forget to take my fish oil tablets this morning. It *kinda* helps me focus.

"And don't call me *Booby*, Buck! Not ever!"

"Uh, sorry, man. What I meant to say was 'Bobby … um … DOOO you know what is down here?'" I said trying to cover up my uh … whatever you'd call what I just did.

"Well how the heck should I know? It could be anything," answered

55

Tiny Tim. "Could be the boiler room, could be a basement."

"Then why a hidden entrance, *bro*? Maybe it's a dungeon and this is where they keep all the kids who don't graduate. And they cut off their heads, like Freddy Krueger."

"For Sloppy Joes!" I said. *"Head cook!* I knew it!"

"Or maybe it's the lab where they make that slop in the first place."

"Maybe it's, *like*, where they made Miss Mary."

We laughed, but to tell you the truth, I think it was more *'cause* we were all nervous than *'cause* it was funny. When we reached the bottom of the stairs, there was a long hallway that seemed to open up into a room with a light coming from it. That's where we headed. The room was big, with lots of little lights around the walls, like computers or something. And in the middle of it all was a bright glowing ball. Like the size of a basketball. It was sort of hovering in the air. At least I couldn't see anything holding it up. And in front of it was the principal, barely able to stand. Slowly he reached up and touched the glowing-orb-thingy. Then the weirdest thing happened. HE started to glow, too!!! Bright!

And there was a strange humming sound. For a second it even looked like he was floating up off the floor. Like he could fly. I don't know if it was cool, or scary. After a minute or two, the light dimmed, and the humming stopped. And then he was able to stand up without holding on. He was strong again. He walked over and looked at the monitors, then went through another doorway and disappeared. Not literally, as in *poof*, I mean he just left the room.

"Awesome!" we all whispered as soon as the door closed. Fred and *Booby*, I mean Fonzie and Bobby, ran over to the glowing thingy. By the time we caught up to them, they were already daring each other to touch it. After about 15 seconds of listening to, "You go first, no *you* go first!" Dex, you know, the guy I call Fonzie, spoke up.

"Let's *all* touch it," he said. Man, I liked him better when he was quiet.

"Hey, everyone, look at these!" yelled Kimmy. *"OMG!* You have got to feel this material!"

"Kimmy, do you realize that you're not actually supposed to say things like *OMG* and *LOL*. That's usually for typing and *IM-ing*. It's *kinda* weird if you ask me," I said.

"Whatever, Buck! But you have to check this out," she said as she took something that looked like a uniform off of a hanger. Did I mention that she had already opened a glass door to get to it? Yeah, she moves pretty fast for a big girl.

"It's soooo soft. Like silk, but it feels really strong, too, like you couldn't rip it if you wanted to. I'm *gonna* try it on."

"Kimmy, that's *gonna* be *wayyyy* too big," said Mina.

"Yeah, even for *you*," I added. Now *that's* funny!

Fonzie thought so, too, 'cause he gave me a thumbs up.

"Oh, you understand my jokes," I said slowly to him, while giving him the thumbs-up sign. Once again, he just frowned and turned away.

So we all stood around and watched Kimmy put on this big uniform because she likes the way it feels. Then when she snapped the belt closed, something really weird happened. Did I say weird, I mean cool. Really cool! We heard a sound like *FFFTTTTTT*. The uniform actually shrunk to fit her. The sleeves, the legs, everything. It was like an invisible tailor came and made it fit perfectly!

Whoa!!!!

"*Ooooh*, here someone take my picture," she said holding out her iPhone.

But we all ran right by her and opened up four more glass cases and took down four more uniforms. We put them on as fast as we could. And just like her, once we snapped the belt closed, we heard *FFFTTTTTT, FFFTTTTTT, FFFTTTTTT, FFFTTTTTT.* That's the sound they made as they shrunk to fit each of us.

"COOL!" we all said.

"The belt buckle looks like one of those *don't-do-something signs.* You know, the circle with the slash through it?"

"Yeah, you're right. And, what's this hanging in the front?" It looked *sorta* like a hood, but like I said it was in the front. As I lifted it up to see what it was for, it

attached to my face and made another *FFFTTTTTT* sound. It scared the mess *outta* me. *"Ahhhhhhhh!* Alien! It's eating my face. It's eating my face!" I screamed.

"Relax, Buck. It's just a mask!"

"Yeah, *bro.* Besides, if it *did* eat your face, I think it might even be an improvement."

That was definitely *not* funny! But I have to admit, his English is a lot better than I thought it was. I found a mirror and looked at myself. This thing covered my whole face. The only thing exposed was my nose and mouth. Oh, and my hair. Which is cool *'cause* like I told you before, the lightning stripe shaved into my hair is my trademark. But it didn't feel like a mask anymore. It was hard, almost like a helmet. I wish I had one of these at home to protect me when I get attacked by my *three-big-mouthed-evil-sisters.* One by one, the others put their masks on, too. It was pretty cool.

"Hey, it *ain't* fabric no more. Now it's hard, like steel. How did it do that?"

We all just *kinda* shrugged our shoulders. You know, that's the I-don't-know-sign.

"*Mira* … I mean look!" said Dex as he put on some weird looking goggles. "How do I look?"

"I like your shades better. Those look like nerd glasses."

"*Yeah,* but I bet they do really cool stuff, like maybe they're infra-red or some *kinda* night vision or thermal vision like in *C.O.D.*"

"Or maybe they're just nerd glasses!" said Kimmy.

"Yo, you play *Call of Duty?*" I asked excitedly.

"Are you kidding, *bro?* I'm a *tenth prestige, level 50!*"

"*For real?!* Do you have a gamer tag?"

"I have one!" said *Booby Boo.*

But I don't think Dex heard me. "Oh, this is so cool," he said, "we look like the Fantastic Four."

"There are five of us, dummy!" said Mina.

"Well then we look like the Fantastic Five, *bro!*"

"Or the Avengers! *C'mon,* let me get some pix of us in the costumes. I can put it on my blog," said Kimmy. "Now be serious, no bunny ears. And no flashing gang signs, Buck!"

"*Whoa!* Hold up, so *'cause* I'm black I have to be in a *gang*? That's *not* funny, Kimmy, that's racist. And I'm not sure that I want a cyber-bully to be posting photos of me on Facebook."

"*SMH*!* I can't take photos! I left my phone in my locker *'cause* they don't let you bring them to detention!" said Kimmy.

"So who's still *down* for touching that glowy thing?" asked Dex.

Dag! I was hoping he forgot about that!

"Well I will if everyone else does," answered Mina.

"Me too," said Kimmy.

"Yeah," said Bobby.

Then they all looked at me. Personally I really didn't want to touch it. But I guess this is what they mean by peer pressure. I had to. Especially since everyone already said they would. How would I look if two girls did it and I didn't? Plus I'm the only black kid, so I'm supposed to be tough. I *gotta* admit, though, I don't always like having to live up to that reputation.

"So, are you *down, bro,* or what?" asked Dex.

"Yeah, of course I'm *down!*" I answered, trying to hide my fear. "I was born *down!* In fact, I'm more *down* than a goose ... get it? Goose down? Anyone?"

"I have a goose down winter coat," piped in Kimmy, "they don't make them any warmer than that. I could go to the North Pole in that coat."

Man, I wish she would. She's *soooo* annoying. In fact, right now I wish I could go to the North Pole to get out of touching this thing. *Dag!* This peer pressure stuff stinks. I *gotta* learn to deal with it a lot better by the time I'm a teenager and folks are trying to get me to drink or smoke.

The worse thing is that if there was anyone else who didn't want to do it, they sure hid it well. Am I really the *only one* who doesn't want to do it? Am I an even bigger *chicken* than the girls? *Sigh* ... that's sad. Maybe I can still talk them out of it. Someone has to be the voice of reason. Or at least the voice of treason.

Here goes nothing. "So what do you think this thing is? How do we even know that it's safe to touch?"

"Who cares?" said Mina. "You saw what it did to the principal. He

---

could barely stand up before he touched it. Then after he stopped glowing he looked like he just drank a carton of Red Bull."

"Well it obviously gave him wings, 'cause the dude looked like he was floating in the air," I said.

"Imagine what I could do with that much power on the four-square court? I might even, *like*, be able to knock someone unconscious with one of my serves," said Mina. "That would be *epic!*"

"Well, I'd like to try it to see if it will make my back feel better. My body still hurts from when *Weggie* fell on top of me." said Bobby.

We all just stared at him.

"I mean Reggie, and it's a long story," he added.

"Well I think something good will happen. It didn't look like it hurt Principal Marshand at all," said Kimmy looking at Bobby. "Who knows, maybe it will even make you grow, little guy … *aaannnnddddd SEND!*"

Fonzie cracked up laughing. *Man!* Okay, I finally get what makes this group laugh. Insults. And the more cruel, the better!

"And maybe it'll make *you* lose weight," little Bobby fired back.

"*Oooohhhh,*" we all said.

Next thing I know Kimmy tries to grab him by the collar like she was trying to pull him towards her. But these uniforms feel like they're glued to our skin so there was nothing to grab ahold of. Then Mina grabbed Bobby around his waist and tried to pull him away. So did Dex. As you can guess, no one wanted to put a hand on Kimmy in fear that she might eat it. Hand, arm, maybe even a leg or two. I took the easy way out and tried to grab her fingers to pry them loose. There we were, in the middle of this giant room that looked like a scene from *Dexter's Laboratory* — the cartoon Dexter, not "Mexican Dexter," — and all they can think about is fighting. No wonder they ended up in detention!

The three of us did our best to pull Bobby away, but with one jerk King-Kong-Kimmy yanked him, and us, forward like we were a bunch of dolls or something. The four of us came flying into her. But when Kimmy tried to brace herself, she stepped on Bobby's soccer ball, and all of us, Kimmy included, went stumbling backwards right into the orb.

Well, I guess we're all going to touch that thing after all!

60

6 3/4

OKAY, SO MAYBE WE SHOULDN'T HAVE TOUCHED THAT THING!"

— *by Buck Bievers*

The glow got brighter and the humming started again. Then *we* started glowing. Remember when I told you that it looked like the principal was floating off the ground? Well I wasn't imagining things because we started floating, too. Even Kimmy, so you *know* this thing is strong if it can pick *her* up. I don't know about the others, but I felt warm and relaxed. Like when your bathroom is cold and you're shivering a bit, then you get in the tub, and it's really warm and it just makes you go *ahhh!* Well, that's *kinda* how it felt. But I felt stronger too. It was great!

After a minute or so, although it was hard to judge, we floated like feathers back down to the ground. Just like we saw the principal do. The light dimmed and the humming stopped.

"WOW!" everyone said at the same time! "That was AWESOME!"

"Yeah but what happened to our uniforms? We're all back in our regular clothes. Where did they go?!"

"*'sta loca,*" said, well by now you should know who always says that.

"Yeah, what happened to those cool costumes?"

"*Awww,* I didn't get a picture of me in *my* costume!" complained Kimmy. It's always about her!

"Yeah, how could they just disappear?"

"I *dunno,* but I know why the principal *digs* this thing, I feel great! My back doesn't hurt anymore, either," said Bobby.

"I wonder why he, *like,* keeps this to himself?" And you know that's Mina *'cause* she can't say a whole sentence without using the word "like."

"I'LL TELL YOU WHY! ..."

Uh-oh! ... Guess who *that* is? Yep, it's the principal. *Dag!* How many times can this guy bust us in *one* day?!! And once again, no one heard him coming.

"This is *not* something for you humans! We have no idea how our technology will interact with your physiology!!!" he yelled.

Ummm ... is it just me, or did the way that he just called us "humans" imply that he is not one of us? *C'mon,* think about it. A girl would never say, "this is not something for *you* girls," because she *is* one, right? Wonder if anyone else picked up on it.

"*You humans?*" repeated Mina. "*Like,* what? ... you're not human?"

"Nah, *bro*, he's a Martian!" said Dex.

"HOW DID YOU KNOW?!" demanded our startled principal.

Uh-oh. I really don't like where this conversation is going. *Please* let him be joking. In fact, if he is joking, I'll be willing to give him my title as *King of Comedy.* But when I looked at his face, there was no smile. Not even one side turned up around the edges.

Dag! This guy is good. Either that ... or ... *gulp* ... he really *is* from Mars.

"*OMG*, you're not *really* a Martian ... are you? *C'mon, LOL!* Right? Say it ... *LOL*. Please? I'll even settle for *JK**," pleaded Kimmy.

"*¡Oye!* Let's examine the facts!" said Dex.

I think that "oye" is Spanish for listen, or shut up or something. That's what I get for doodling during Spanish class. And did that sentence really come out of his mouth? "Let's examine the facts?" He didn't even use the word "bro" this time. I can't wait to hear what his facts are. But I'll bet they're *gonna* be pretty dumb.

"Okay, fact number one," Dex continued, "Just look at him, there's something about him that just looks a little different. You can't quite put your finger on it, but it's there, right?"

Everyone nodded.

Bobby added, "And, did you ever notice how you never hear him coming? Right?" I don't know if he doesn't make a sound when he walks, or he teleports like in Star Track."

"Trek," Dex corrected.

"That's what I said, okay?"

"No, you said *track* like a race track. But it's Star TREK. A trek is a journey," said Dex. "And you're right, he doesn't make a sound. But that doesn't make him an alien. Some people walk quietly, some are loud."

We all looked at Kimmy.

"WhatEVER!" Kimmy shot back.

"Okay," said Dex. "Ever see him laugh? And I don't just mean at your lame jokes, Buck or Duck or whatever your name is, 'cause no one laughs at them anyhow."

Dag! He *dissed* me and just kept right on talking.

"And what about how you never see him go to the bathroom?

Hmmm, that's kind of a good point, but there are a lot of folks I've never seen go to the bathroom. Like Justin Beiber, for example. But does that make *him* an alien? … Although that would explain a lot.

"Aw-ight, here's a good one," continued Dex, "no matter what the weather is, he always wears the same thing. A white shirt, red tie and a sports jacket. It could be like 10 degrees outside and he don't *never* have a coat on."

"Dexter!" interrupted the principal. If you're going to stand there and accuse me of being from another planet, *at least* don't do it with a double negative. You should have said 'he doesn't ever have a coat on.'"

I have to admit, Fonzie was right about everything, except for the double-negative part. But then, my Uncle Donnie is the same way. Only instead of a jacket and tie, he wears a Derek Jeter Yankee jersey. Whether it's two degrees or 110 degrees, you can bet he's got on that shirt. And man, it's probably older than Jeter himself. I know that's impossible, but just go with it. Plus he wears a Red Sox cap, which is just insane. Now Uncle Donnie lives upstate with a bunch of other people who are just like him.

"I *ain't* done yet, *bro*."

"Dexter!" yelled the Principal.

"Oh yeah, sorry. I am *not* done yet."

"That's better, you may continue."

Dex added more to his case, "Anyone here ever see him eat? Ever? I mean you see him in the cafeteria at lunch, but he *don't* never … I mean he doesn't ever eat."

Well that's not my Uncle Donnie. He looks like he ate half the Yankee lineup and saved Robinson Cano for dessert. Must weigh about 400 pounds.

"Think about it. Raise your hand if you've ever seen this guy eat?"

"He had a strawberry yogurt for lunch today!" I added.

"And you saw him eat it?" asked Dex.

"Nah, but his shirt sure seemed to like it," I added.

Dex just turned away and continued his thought. "And what about you, Miss iPhony?" he said pointing to Kimmy. "If anyone knows, it would be you *'cause* you spend more time in the cafeteria than Miss Mary."

"WhatEVER!" snapped Kimmy again.

Now *that's* funny! So was iPhony. I wish I had said them both, except that she'd probably be beating me to a pulp right now.

"Hey, I'm just *sayin'*, you go back for seconds almost every day! And I even see you puttin food in your bag sometimes."

"You're a liar!" yelled Kimmy. And when I say that she yelled, I mean she *yelled*. That was intense, even for her. Wonder what *that's* about?

"Yeah, well those are all good facts, Dexter," said Mina trying to stop everyone from staring at Kimmy, "but we're overlooking the obvious stuff. First of all, *like*, who in their right mind would eat in our cafeteria if they didn't have to? But, look around, we're standing in a hidden part of the school, surrounded by all these computers that don't look anything like the crappy stuff we have to use in tech class. Plus to top it off, he just, *like*, touched a glowing orb that lifted him up off the ground and seemed to heal whatever was wrong with him. Yeah, it's interesting that no one has ever seen him eat, but the man owns a *glowing orb!!!*"

"And even his name ... Marshand? All he did was add a 'D' to Martian! What could be more obvious," added Fonzie or Fred, or whatever I was calling him now. You know, I'm starting to think that Dex isn't nearly as dumb as we think he is. He may not even be as dumb as *he* thinks he is.

"Okay, Principal Marshand ..." perked up Bobby, "... you always tell us not to cheat, or steal or lie. So now it's your turn. Are you an alien? And I don't mean from Mexico like Dexter, or someplace else on Earth. I mean, are you from another planet?"

"I keep telling you, I'm *not* Mexican, I'm Puerto Rican!" yelled Dex.

"Whatever," said Mina. Principal Marshand slowly looked each of us in the eyes. Then he took a deep breath and opened his mouth to say something. And that something was ...

We'll have his answer after this commercial break. Don't you hate when you're watching one of those talent shows, like American Idol or whatever, and just when they get ready to announce who's going home they go to a commercial? It drives me nuts. They take forever, then they still make you wait. *Man*, that makes me mad. Oh, sorry, you're waiting for his answer, aren't you? Well here it is, the answer is ... Ready? ... Here it comes ...

"Yes!"

I thought I was standing too close to the orb, because suddenly I had that same warm feeling that I had when we were all glowing. I closed my eyes and waited to be picked up off the ground again. But nothing happened. Then I realized that it wasn't all of me that was warm. Just my legs. Strange. I wonder why that is? Then I realized that the warm feeling wasn't from the orb, it was from my bladder. *Dag!*

"I knew it!" said Bobby. "I knew you were a Martian! You had to be! All that stuff the Mexican kid said, plus I just felt it. It was like my Spidey-Sense or something."

"I'm NOT Mexican, I'm Puerto Rican!" said Dex.

"Same thing!" said Bobby.

"No it's not, and what, like being Japanese is better, *bro?*"

"Dude, I'm NOT Japanese, I'm Korean!"

"SAME THING!" snarled Dex.

That was a good one! But I wanted to get everyone back on track.

"C'mon, guys, can we get back to the fact that our principal is a real-live Martian?" Then I turned to look at him. So, you're really from Mars?" I finally said as I took off my hoodie and wrapped it around my soaking-wet pants before anyone noticed. "What's it like?"

"Do they have iPhones on Mars?" asked you-know-who.

"Are you here to invade Earth, or do you come in peace?" asked Mina. "You're not going to eat us, are you?"

"If you are," I said, "do yourself a favor and start with Kimmy, she's got enough meat on her bones to last you *'til* next semester. You won't even have to eat the rest of us. In fact, you may never have to eat again. You could probably even ship the leftovers back to feed your family on Mars."

She growled in my direction. Either that or it was her stomach telling her it was time for lunch again.

"*Uh-oh,* maybe *she's* the one who's *gonna* eat us!" I said.

Dex cracked up! I'm starting to like him.

Anyway, fifteen minutes ago, the five of us were in detention. Now, we're in some hidden room of the school with our Martian principal, hoping that we won't all be eaten. Talk about a day taking a turn for the worse.

"So what happens now?" someone asked. I'm not really sure who is asking what at this point. Between learning that my principal is an alien, and trying to hide the fact that I wet my pants, my mind is a bit preoccupied. I mean, this is the *kinda* thing that could last a lifetime and have a major effect on one's life. I mean the *peeing-in-the-pants* thing, not the Martian thing. They still call one of my dad's friends *Stinky* because of something that happened to him in high school. And he's like 40 years old! So if someone finds out that I wet my pants, they might start calling me something that will stick with me for the rest of my life, too! Something like *Buck Pee-vers* or *Pee-Diddy!* Or I'll have to hear jokes like, 'Hey, Buck, I used to think that you were African American, but now I know *You're-a-peein'.*" (Get it, *European*?) It's *kinda* weird that I just found out my principal is a Martian and that's not the biggest secret in my life right now.

"Well, I can't just let you leave," said the Martian.

"I knew it! I knew he was going to eat us! Everyone run! Except for you, Kimmy. You stay here and volunteer to be the first course!"

"First COURSES!" someone added.

"I do *not* eat humans," snapped the offended alien.

"Not even our brains?" I asked timidly.

"Well if I do eat brains, none of you will have anything to worry about!" he snapped.

Yo! Now I'm being *dissed* by a Martian with no sense of humor. I *gotta* admit, I like the way he keeps a straight face. He's really dry, but he can also be funny. *Kinda* like Peyton Manning. Makes it look like he knows he's so funny that he doesn't need to laugh at his own jokes. I'd love to be able to do that. But it's hard since I'm so funny I even make myself laugh.

"As I was saying, I do not plan to eat you, nor do you any harm. But we do need to talk before I can let you go."

"Will you, *like*, erase our memories, like in *Men in Black*?"

"No."

"Well can you at least erase the black kid's corny sense of humor? What's your name again, Bucky?" asked Fonzie.

"Buck," I said. "Buck Peevers."

"Did you just say PEE-vers?" asked Kimmy and Bobby at the same time.

"No, no, no! I said BIEVERS, I swear. B-I-E-V-E-R-S!" *Man,* that was close. I almost gave myself away.

Suddenly the principal waved his hand and a light went on in a far corner of the room. Cool. There was a table, with chairs around it. He motioned for us to go over and take a seat. Everyone walked towards the table but kept an eye on him in case he was planning to pull out a light saber or something.

And then he started talking:

"Yes, I *am* from the planet Mars. Yes, I know, how *cliche.* And I'm not alone. Thousands of your years ago, Mars was much like Earth. We had water, trees, or at least our version of trees and various creatures. And even a breathable atmosphere. But through senseless acts of war, and our own arrogance, we destroyed it. Much like you are doing to your planet. As a result, without the protection of our atmosphere, our only chance for survival was to flee the planet, which was difficult, or to move underground, which is what many of us did."

"Like the movie Journey to the Center of the Earth," shouted someone.

"You mean, Journey to the Center of Mars!" added Kimmy.

"Or am I thinking about City of Ember? Whatever, they were both terrible!"

"Anyway, fortunately for us, our scientists developed the life orbs that you have just discovered."

"*Ummm* ... excuse me, Principal Marshand, but is there going to be a test on this later?"

"Shut up, Bobby!" snapped Mina.

"No, I just want to know if we need to be taking notes or something."

"Yeah, while you're at it, you can take notes for Dexter, too," said Mina. "And if we get homework, I'm sure he won't mind if you do it for him."

"*Yo,* forget you, Mina!" yelled Dex.

"Let me get this straight, I am in the process of admitting that I am from Mars, but you interrupt me in order to argue?"

"Sorry, sir. Please continue."

"That's better. Where was I? Yes, We came here to try to cultivate your life forms in order for them to survive on our planet. We sampled everything, from your atmosphere to your plants, and tried to come up with strains that will live on our home world."

"Take Mina. Please!"

"Whatever, *loser*. So, *like*, what does the orb do?"

"The orbs alter our physiology so that we can survive on your planet."

"Can somebody Google *fizzy-o-lo-gee*?"

"It means your body and stuff."

"I still don't know what *cliche* means."

He ignored us, "The orbs change our bodies so that we're able to breathe your air; eat your disgusting food; drink your water; heal our wounds; and adapt to your gravity. That's the good part."

"What's the bad part? Migraines ... foot fungus ... gas?"

"The bad part is that unfortunately, I have no idea of what it will do to *you*. But I do know this, you did not properly prepare before tapping into the power of the orb."

"What do you mean prepare? Like homework? *'Cause* I ain't doing no homework. I don't care if it gives me x-ray vision," said Dex.

"*Sigh* ... the orb unites our body, mind and what you call soul or spirit. If we have strong minds and weak bodies, the orb will use the strength of our mind to help build a stronger body. If your strength is your spirit, the orb will tap into its power to increase your mental capacity. And if you take care of all three, the orb will help you to become a complete individual; one who is capable of operating at their fullest capacity. That's why I need so little food, or rest. And my demeanor is one of tranquility and peace. But you! You five are bullies. You pick on kids who you feel are inferior to you. You hurt them physically. You hurt them mentally. You tease them until they cry. Then you drink up their tears like the juice of an apple. But even as bad as you treat others, the individuals whom you treat the worst ... are yourselves."

"What? I know you're not talking about me! I just bought myself a new Abercrombie shirt and a a pair of Uggs. I think I treat myself just fine!"

said Kimmy.

He said nothing. Instead he just stared at her.

"They're … ummm … boots," she added shyly. "You know, Uggs … they're boots."

"I'm aware of that, Miss Kampbell. Yes, the world can see what you wear on your outside. But what is going on inside of you?"

"Well, I'll bet there's enough room inside her to play four-square," *oooh*, that's gotta be my best line of the day.

"We'll get to you in a minute, Mr. Bievers. The food you kids eat has made you a victim of childhood obesity."

"O.B. City? Where's that?" asked Dex.

"It's the capital of Cupcake Land. It's ruled by Mayor McCheese."

"Forget you, Ducky!" shot back Dex.

"Obesity. And do you see? You can't go ten seconds without trying to tear each other down. No wonder none of you have any self-esteem anymore. It's constantly under attack. If you take away a brick every day, after a while, even the sturdiest building will collapse. Kids today are not like they used to be when I first came here. You are young, but you do not run and exercise. You are around other kids your age, but you do not play with them. You have so much, but you do not share. You live in the house with brothers and sisters who you refuse to attempt to get along with. Siblings who you don't even treat as well as your classmates, and they share your same blood in their veins. And most of all, you go to school, but you refuse to learn. You make your teachers' jobs ten times as hard as they should be. And they're here to help you. Do you think that anyone ever becomes a teacher because they hate kids?"

"Well, I'll bet Mr. Vetter did!"

The principal shot Mina an evil look.

"What? He's terrible. Besides, he smells like old cigars! *Ugh!* I'd rather he fail me than breathe on me!" she answered back.

"That can be arranged!" Principal M. continued, "As I was saying, even though you know that now is when you need to begin to lay down the foundation of your future, you don't properly prepare yourselves. I'm glad the orb did not try to make you whole, as negative as your minds are, you might be transformed into hideous monsters."

"He's right! Look at Mina!" I shouted. "Oh no, it's too late, she already *is* a hideous monster!"

"You're, *like*, such an *epic fail*, Buck!"

"Children, please! You must promise me that you will not breathe a word of this to anyone. It will jeopardize my safety, and maybe even yours!"

"Okay, so, *like*, what if we promise? Then what?"

"Then you're free to go. But I want you to take my cell phone number and if you feel any ill effects from the orb, please call me immediately."

"But they're really nice boots."

"Excuse me, Miss Kampbell?"

"My Uggs. Remember? They're really nice boots. They're like these, but in black. I'll wear them tomorrow. '*K*'?"

"Miss Kampbell, I do not care about your boots. I care about you."

"Whatever," Kimmy sighed.

"You're free to go."

You know, in all the excitement, the one thing that none of us asked him about was what happened to those cool uniforms that we tried on. How did we get back in our regular clothes? It's like they just disappeared. It was weird. Even the glasses that Dex tried on. Too bad, they *really* were cool. The uniforms, not the glasses.

Definitely *not* the glasses!

Man, I can't wait to get home to change my pants.

7
PRIDE VERSUS JOY!
— by Mina Madsen

It was about 4:15 when my Dad pulled up in the circle to pick me up. He had to wait for the car in front of him to pull off, so it gave me time to take off my chain, wrap it up and put it back in my pocket. "You're late!" I said as I opened the car door and threw in my backpack.

"Sorry, honey. Daddy had a job interview today. How was school? Anything exciting happen?"

"Well, if you absolutely must know, I found out that my principal is a Martian," I said. I don't know what happened, but when I said that, it was like I got an electric shock. Not a big one, but like when you rub your feet on a carpet then touch your ear or something.

"That's nice, baby," said my dad, who obviously wasn't listening to me… as usual.

"No, really, he's, *like*, from another planet!" I added. But once again, for the reaction he gave me, I could have said that my head was about to pop off and he *still* wouldn't have heard me. "Dad, tonight after you and Mom go to bed, I'm going to pack my bags and run away from home. And you'll never see me again. Ever!"

"That's GREAT!!!" He yelled at the top of his lungs.

"What? You WANT me to run away?" I asked nervously.

"Yes, and the sooner the better."

"But, Daddy! …"

Then he turned around, put one finger to his lips and made that *shush* sound.

"Daddy's on the phone, Mina. Give me a minute, will you? — Sorry, my daughter was talking to me, but yes, the sooner we can arrange a follow-up meeting, the better."

Ugh! He's on his stupid cell phone again. And he always wears his headset in his left ear, so I can never see it when he talks in the car. So sometimes I've had whole conversations with him, or at least I thought it was with him, and he wasn't even talking to me. Looks like that's what just happened again. You know what? If I *did* run away, I wonder how long it would take Mom and Dad to even notice? But if my sister Joy takes too long in the bathroom, they're both ready to call the FBI to start a nationwide search.

That's right, my mom is just as bad. Sometimes we'll be at the dinner table and they'll both be talking on the phone or answering email at the same time. Once, I went into the other room and called my dad on his cell. When he answered, I just said "Hi, Daddy, it's me, Mina … you know, your daughter? I don't mean to disturb your *important* phone call, but will you please pass me the mashed potatoes?"

He didn't think it was all that funny. He said I interrupted one of his important business calls. My father could be talking to Domino's Pizza and he'd *still* say the call was "life or death." Sure, the kids at school all think that it's cool that my mom and dad know how to IM and text and all of that stuff. My mom even *Tweets*. But believe me, it's no big deal. Usually on TV shows it's the kids who are texting and the parents who want them to stop so they can all talk "as a family." But not in my house. My folks are, *like*, totally *plugged in*. Too much, if you ask me.

Ten minutes later we pull up at my sister's school. I don't know about her, but I'm glad we don't go to the same school. The car door swings open and Joy pops her big head in.

"Hi, Daddy. Hi, Mina," she says all bubbly and stuff. She's always *sooooooo* happy, it's amazing that we have the same parents. Plus, we're *twins*. Not identical, thank goodness. But we couldn't be any more different if we tried. And not like peanut butter and jelly, 'cause although they're different, at least they still go together. We're more like peanut butter and soap powder!

"I really like your nails, Mina. That red really looks good on you. And I like how you leave the two ring fingers black. It's cool."

I just looked the other way without saying a word. But my father? Oh, no, of course he wouldn't let his precious little *Joy* enter without making a big deal over it.

"*Gotta* go," said Dad. Then he pressed the button on his headset to hang up the call. Hey! Why didn't he get off his precious phone when *I* got in the car?

"Guess what, Joy? Daddy just got a call back on my job interview, and they want me to come in for a second meeting!"

"That's great, Daddy!" shrieked Joy. *Ugh!* I *hate* that little cutesy-pie scream that she does. It's *soooo* fake.

"Daddy?" she said again. "Have you seen my heart necklace?"

"You mean the one that I gave you for winning the talent show?"

"Yes, that's the one. I haven't seen it in a few days. Do you have any idea where it might be?"

"No, *puddin'*, I don't. But we can all help you look for it when we get home. Won't we, Mina?"

"Sorry, *puddin',*" I mocked, "I won't have time to help look for your precious little locket. I've got tons of homework. Maybe you should just be more careful where you put things!" Then I placed my head against the window of the car and just *sorta* zoned out. Dad and Joy talked the whole ride, but I couldn't tell you what they said. Meanwhile, I spent the time thinking about this whole Martian thing and how I hoped that everything would work out.

I mean what would *you* do if you found out your principal was from another planet? Would you tell your parents? Would you call the police? The FBI? The army? And if you did, would anyone believe you? Or would you keep it a secret like he asked you to do? I mean, he seems nice enough and all. And he didn't mention any plot to, *like*, destroy the Earth. So I guess we're safe.

But boy, if they do blow up the Earth, I'm gonna feel *really* guilty about not warning anyone. Although I did try to tell my Dad, so technically I guess it will be *his* fault. I sat in silence until we pulled into our driveway. I didn't say a word the whole ride. I just sat quietly, stroking the links of the chain in my pocket.

8

THE SK8 PARK
— by Dexter Diaz

Well so much for detention being boring! Man, if it was always like this, detention would be my favorite part of school. I'd be doing stuff all the time just to get sent there. The teacher would be like, "Dex, did you do your homework today?" and I'd be like, "No! I made that nerdy kid over there do it for me." Then she'd say, "In that case, Dex, you'll need to go to detention." And I'd be like, "Aw-ight, I'm there!"

So, my principal is an alien. And the worst part is I can't tell *nobody*. I don't know if it's *'cause* I promised him, or if I'm afraid that if he finds out he'll beam into my room in the middle of the night and eat my brain. Not that I'd miss it.

All my life I've heard stuff like, "Dex ain't the sharpest knife in the drawer," and other clever ways to call me a dummy. Not like my little cousin Papito. Man, that kid can sneeze and everyone is, like, "Wow, did you see the way he sneezed? He's a genius!" Oh well, at least I ain't *gotta* worry about none of the kids here calling me names to my face. They know how strong I am and that I'd pound them into tomorrow.

As soon as I walk out the door to the middle school, I see Hayden Parker about to get on the bus. If I wasn't so freaked out over this whole Martian thing, I'd go over and *let him have it* for doing *my* homework on *his* stationery. For someone who's supposed to be so smart, that sure was a stupid thing to do. Hey … unless he *wanted* to get caught. Or at least he wanted *me* to get caught. Well it worked, so maybe he's not so dumb after all. Maybe I was the dummy for not looking it over before I handed it in.

I shoot an *I'll-talk-to-you-later stare* at him, then head around to the side of the school to get my bike off the rack. Hayden runs to the back of the bus, then ducks behind a seat in case I decide to come after him. All I want is my bike. Some of the kids lock theirs up, but I never do. It's my way of daring someone to mess with it.

You know what's funny? One of the best things about having a *rep* (reputation) as a tough kid is that you never actually have to fight. That's *'cause* everyone assumes that you fight all the time and that you're always ready to give someone a *beatdown*. *'sta loca*, right? But to tell you the truth, the last fight I got in was four years ago with my cousin *Flaco* tried to steal one of my FIFA video games.

So now I just play up the whole strong, silent-type thing. Freaks people out. Kids are afraid of me. Teachers don't know what to make of me. Which all in all, really *ain't* so bad … I guess.

77

Dex

I put my skateboard on the rack of my bike, then head over to the park to hang out with the freaks. I don't like taking the school bus, and no one ever comes to pick me up from school. Not that I'd ever want my dad to drive up in our old car and park in between all of those gigantic SUVs. Man, some of those things are as big as a bus! The cool part about the freaks at the park is that no one pretends to be anything they're not. So they don't even *try* to get any closer to you than they already are. No phone calls, no texting and no play dates (even though only the nerds still call them that). They don't invite you to their birthday party, and you never have to meet them at the movies or the mall. Plus you don't ever have to worry about them *blowin' up your IM* the second you go online.

We come. We hang out. We leave. What could be simpler? There are even a couple of girls who hang out at the park. And let me tell you, *bro*, they're even weirder than the guys. Colored streaks in their hair, tattoos … One girl even has a few piercings. One in her tongue, and *yo*, one is in her finger, just above the knuckle. *Ewwww!* That just freaks me out. In fact, out of all the kids I've met here, the only time I ever talked to one of them at home is on Xbox Live. A couple of the freaks are really into C.O.D.

Know what else is weird? Most of these kids' families have more money than Santa Claus. That's dumb, I probably *shoulda* said Oprah or that Will Gates guy, you know, the dude who made Microsoft. Will … Bill … something like that. How can you be miserable when your folks are rich? I just don't get it. Listen to this, so my dad owns an auto shop and he doesn't want me to ever work for him. But some of these guys' dads have multi-million dollar companies and are *dying* for their kids to follow in their footsteps. But their kids don't want any part of them. They'd rather be poor than to be like their dads. It's crazy! I mean *'sta loco!*

By the time I get to the park, there's already about five kids there. One of them was obviously waiting for me, *'cause* as soon as he saw me, his face lit up and he started walking towards me. It's definitely not cause we're *BFFs* or nothing like that. I'll bet his bike is jacked up and he needs me to work my magic. As he gets closer, I see the chain is dangling from the pedals. Man, I can't believe he can't fix that himself. But, you know what's even worse? Why is he riding an old piece of crap like that anyway? His folks are so rich they probably blow their noses with 50 dollar bills. If that was my family, you can bet my bike would be *official**! I'd ride down the street and heads would turn.

*Check out the definition of *official* in the back of the book.

I keep a mini toolkit in my backpack, so it was easy to fix his bike. When I was done, he reached in his bag and pulled out a couple of Xbox games. I check 'em out, then pick the one I want as *payment*. If I don't like it, I can always trade it in at GameStop to get a store credit. Then when I have enough saved up, I can get a game that I *really* want. While we're sitting there, a few of the other freaks come and sit next to us. No one really saying much, just stuff like, "Check out this song on my iPod," or, "Look at this game I downloaded on my phone," or "Watch me do this *sick* trick on my skateboard or bike." Little things like that. While I'm sitting there, I start to wonder if I can tell these guys about the whole *my principal is a Martian thing*.

What do *you* think I should do?

Okay, I'm *gonna* do it. I mean, if anyone will believe me, it's *gotta* be these weirdoes, right? So finally there was a silence. No one was talking at all. Might as well just blurt it out, so I do.

"My principal is an alien!"

Ow! What the heck was that? Something shocked me.

More silence.

Finally the kid with the dirty hair spoke up. Well that could be all of them, so change that to the kid with the dirtiest hair said, "You mean, like from Mexico?"

Then the others joined in. "Isn't that where you're from? And is he here illegally? *Yo*, you should definitely report him. But make sure they don't send your family back, too."

"Does he have a green card?"

"They sent my nanny back. I think it was to Honduras, or Columbia, or somewhere. I came home from school one day and she was gone. She didn't even get a chance to make dinner first. We had to order take-out all week. Plus, they didn't even let her take her dog with her, so it still lives with us."

"Nah, *bro*," I said, "He's like, you know, from Mars and stuff. And I'm *not* Mexican, I was born here, just like you clowns!"

"*Jeez*, that's wild," says one of them. "*Kinda* hard to believe."

"Yeah, right?" I say, happy that they believe me.

"You were born *here*?" he asks. *Aw*, man, he was talking about *me!* "Of course I was born here," I snapped. "Didn't you hear me, I said my *freakin'* principal is a *freakin'* Martian!" *Buzzzz* ... another shock. What the heck is happening to me? What keeps shocking me?!

"*Ohhhhhhh*, a Martian! We thought you meant like an illegal alien. That's different," said the kid whose bike I fixed.

More silence.

Then they started up again. "Well, I know what you mean, 'cause I think my principal is a robot! Man, he's *so* stiff. He walks like his underwear is too tight."

"Dude, mine is a like baboon or somethin'. He's short, and his hair is even *sorta* orange. *Kinda* smells a little funny, too. Like old bananas."

Now that they're talking, I really miss the silence. I block them out by reading the back of the Xbox game. Only one player, Xbox Live ... that's good.

"Well my principal is like a Pit Bull. Boy, is he tough!"

After another minute or so, I put the game in my bag, then get on my bike to leave.

"That was fun, Dex, next we can talk about what kind of animals our dads are or something," one of them yelled as I rode off.

"Yeah, mine is like a gorilla, only without the hair."

Sigh ... Guess I'll head home.

9
THE MINIVAN
— *by Kimmy Kampbell*

"*OMG!* What is this you're driving, Mom?"

"What do you mean, Kimmy, it's the minivan?"

"I thought you were getting the BMW back! You promised!"

"No, *you* promised! Kimmy, we've been over this a thousand times! The BMW is your *father's* car. When he moved in with his new girlfriend and her kids, he took it with him. Along with most of our savings, I might add! Got it? We're lucky he let us keep this minivan. Everything was in *his* name. Remember that, Kimmy, *always* get stuff put in your name. It makes it legal. You'll thank me one day when your husband leaves *you* for another woman."

"But can't you ask Dad if you can use it just to pick me up from school, Mom?"

"Kimmy, the BMW is your father's car. Case closed!!! Look around, lots of people here drive minivans, we're not the only ones!"

"I know, but it's just not as cool, or as fancy."

"But it's big and the seats fold down. Kimmy, just get in! PLEASE!"

"*Sigh* ... whatever."

So I got in the stupid minivan, closed the door, and slid down in my chair so I wouldn't be seen. Mom talked about a bunch of stuff. Some of it I heard, some of it I didn't. I just looked out the window without saying a word. The next thing I knew, we were pulling up into the parking lot of the supermarket. "*C'mon*, Kimmy, I just have to pick up a few things."

I hate going shopping. Well, I hate going shopping for *food*. But I *love* shopping for clothes. We got out the van and took a few steps when my mom stopped in her tracks.

"*Oops*, almost forgot."

Oh no, please, not *that*!

"Mommy can't forget her coupon book! Triple savings today. Every penny counts, you know," she says smiling.

Ugh, how embarrassing. Ever since my dad moved out, my mom has become a real cheapskate!!! Coupons, discount stores, and the worst part is that when I ask her for stuff now, sometimes she says, "No!"

It's just not fair. And now my dad talks about how he has to watch his money because he has to pay rent for his new apartment in the city. And, to make it worse, he used to visit every weekend. Then it was every other weekend. Now it's like, once a month, if I'm lucky. I heard Mom, on the phone, tell one of her friends that she thinks my dad is *gonna* marry his stupid girlfriend. Then he'll have three new kids. That stinks! What about me?

We go to the deli counter and take a number. What will it be today? Bologna? Sliced turkey? Can we get cheese this time?! When our order is ready, mom asks the guy behind the counter for a few paper plates, plastic utensils and napkins. Then she looks at her list and we walk to pick up a few more things. Bottled water, juice boxes ... Doesn't matter what the brand is, the only thing that matters is if it's on sale. And nothing that's going to spoil, like milk. That's why we only buy enough meat to make a few sandwiches at a time. Then comes the part I hate the most about grocery shopping with Mom — going to the back corners of the store. That's because on one side they keep "yesterday's baked goods." That's where they sell stuff like bread and pies for half price because they're already a day old. She loves going through this rack. To her it's like Christmas!

"Oooh, look at these nice sandwich rolls," she says to me like she's holding up a winning lottery ticket. "And they're still soft. *Whaddaya* say, should we live it up?"

"Sure, Mommy," I say as dry as I can. *"Yipeee!"*

Next we head to the other corner *'cause* that's where they put the fruit and veggies that are also a *little* on the old side, but a *lot* on the cheap side.

"Only one small brown spot on this pear. Apples look decent, too," she says.

I shoot her a *can-we-go-now look*, so she hurries up and puts the moldy fruit in our cart and we head to the check-out counter.

"Mommy, can I have this please?" I ask while holding up a Teen Vogue.

"No, Kimmy, not today. It's not in ..."

"I know, *it's not in the budget!*" I snap. Nothing's ever in our lousy budget anymore.

Daddy, if you can hear me, wherever you are ...

I *hate* you!

10
GET ON THE BUS

— by Buck Bievers

I got on the bus and saw Bobby sitting in the back. I couldn't wait to talk to him.

"So, what do you think?"

"About what, *dude?*"

Okay, so Bobby and I just found out that the principal of our school is from another planet, and he doesn't know what I'm talking about?

"About Principal Marshand! What do you think, Bobby?"

"Oh, I *dunno.* What do you think?"

"I don't know either. Are you *gonna* tell your mom?"

"I don't think so. Besides, no one will ever believe us. Don't you watch movies? Adults *never* believe kids about stuff like this. Ever!"

He's right. I can imagine telling my mom or dad. Or even worse, the monster known as my *three-big-mouthed-evil-sisters*. They'd tease me for the rest of my life. I'd have to run away from home. Man, this is one of the worst days of my life. I can't even think of anything funny to say. So I don't say anything. Neither does Bobby. So we sit and say nothing for the rest of the ride. We must have looked weird since we were probably the only two kids on the bus who weren't bouncing on the seats or throwing stuff. I just looked out the window. This was going to be the longest bus ride of my life.

Know what's funny? — Not ha-ha funny, but strange funny — The law is that when you ride in a car, you have to wear a seat belt, right? But do you know the one place where kids *don't* have to buckle up? On a school bus! You'd think that would be the one place where they'd make us, right? Adults and their stupid laws!

"Smell that?" he asked.

"What?" I asked back.

"Smells like one of the little kids peed their pants again."

"Oh yeah, that's what little kids do." I said while praying he doesn't realize that it's me.

So what do we do now?" he asked me.

"*Wanna* play the new Angry Birds on my phone?" I asked.

"Sure!" So we did.

THE "MAD"-SENS
— by Mina Madsen

Dinner is always the same in my house. We sit in the *same* places. Use the *same* dishes. And have the *same* boring conversation in between my mom and dad's business calls and texts. Then we all sit around and listen to Joy talk about her boring day — almost minute-by-minute. Then everyone gets mad at me for rolling my eyes or sighing. They say it's "disrespectful." Tonight didn't matter though, because I was busy thinking about everything that happened today. Just think, a few hours ago, my biggest problem was that I got out in four-square. Now it's what to do about my Martian principal.

I didn't feel like eating, especially since we had salmon for dinner. I don't like fish, but no one seems to ever remember that. Plus the stuff that we have is always so fancy. I'd give anything to have something simple every once in a while. Even meatloaf. You know what's funny? Our cafeteria meatloaf isn't half bad. In fact, I *kinda* like it. They usually serve it with corn, which I also like. But the main veggies that I get here at home are stuff like asparagus and Brussels sprouts. *Yuck!* But even though I wasn't hungry, I couldn't stop drinking. We're only allowed to have water during dinner, so I had, *like*, four glasses. Weird, huh?

I don't even know what they talked about today, or even IF they talked at all. I zoned out for most of it, because I was too busy thinking about what to do. I'm sure it was probably the same as it always is. My mom talked about her lawyer stuff. — What case she's working on, and how she had to confront one of her coworkers who did something she didn't like. Then Dad probably talked about his search for a job. I'm sure he gave the details of that phone conversation he had when he picked me up. After dinner I did my homework, which I also don't really remember doing. It was like I was in a trance. By the time 9:30 came around, I was *really* sleepy, so I went to bed. First I had two more glasses of water! Boy, I'm going to be up all night *peeing*. I know that some kids like to stay up late and stuff, but sometimes I can't wait to go to sleep so the day will be over.

This is one of those days!

12

TWISTED SISTERS

— *by Buck Bievers*

I got off the bus and walked down the driveway to my house. The garage door was open, so I went in through there. It was bad enough that I got sent to detention *and* found out that my principal is from another planet — then I wet my pants — but *now* I have to face the most hideous creature ever known to man: the three-headed T-Rex — my *three-big-mouthed-evil-sisters:* Taylor, Trina and Tammy.

As soon as I opened the door, the first thing I hear is the first thing that I *always* hear … arguing! Usually something like, "Take it off now, Trina!"

"Oh, like you never take stuff out of *my* closet, Taylor? And you're wearing my bracelet right now!"

That's the way they do with each other. Hour after hour, day after day, year after year! And there's only one thing that stops them from picking on each other …

"Well what are you looking at, *twerp*?!"

"Yeah, what do *you* want, Buck?!"

Yep, you guessed it … it's me! The only thing that keeps them from picking on each other is having me around for all three of them to pick on. It's like having a common enemy (namely me) is the only thing they can agree on. I know I'm going to get picked on the rest of the night, so I come out swinging.

"If I were your sister, I would *never* borrow your clothes without asking first, Taylor."

"See? Even the *twerp* knows that it's common courtesy not to just take stuff out of someone's closet. And he's got as much manners as a wild hog!"

"No, I just wouldn't look good in an extra, extra large," I said.

"What? Are you saying this skirt makes me look fat?"

"No, I think my eyes are what makes you look fat!" I shoot back!

"Why you little …"

Time to run. Now here's the part I don't get. The only one I insulted was Taylor, so why are all three of them chasing me around the house? That's why I call them the "three-headed-monster."

I dashed through the kitchen door, into the living room and around the couch. A great move if there was only one of them. Maybe even two.

But it's hard to get away from all three of them. And they're no dummies either, but don't tell them I said so. They must be on to my couch trick because as soon as they get to it, Taylor and Tammy go to the right while Trina follows me to the left. I turn to head towards the stairs, if I can just make it up the steps, I can lock myself in my room until my parents get home. But before I can make it, I hear a *thud!* Actually I *feel* a thud. That was me slamming against our hardwood floor. Did I just get tackled? By Tammy? But she's only six! Yep! That's what happened all right.

Next thing I know I'm being dragged by my feet back into the kitchen.

"Get the scarves from the closet! And take that stupid hoodie from around his waist!"

And so they did.

"Ewwwwww, Buck peed his pants!"

"Gross!"

Sigh ... as if my day wasn't already bad enough ..."

I hear footsteps running towards the hall closet while two sets of hands lift me up and put me in a kitchen chair. Dag! The least they could let me do is change my pants!

But no such luck.

Well at least they're not arguing anymore.

1 IN 7 STUDENTS IN GRADES K-12 IS EITHER A BULLY OR A VICTIM OF BULLYING.
— DoSomething.org

12³/₄

CHAIRMAN OF THE BORED

(Get it, I'm in a chair and I'm bored!
Man, even my chapter titles are funny!)
— by a really embarrassed and soaking wet Buck Bievers

It was about 6:30 p.m. when I heard my dad's car pull up in the driveway. That means that I've been tied up in this chair for about two hours. *TWO HOURS!!!*

I hear the front door open and in walk Mom and Dad.

"Oh, Buck!" says my mom, "What did you do to your sisters *this time?*"

"He's got a scarf around his mouth, dear," says my dad.

"Oh for heaven's sake," she says as she pulls the scarf down so I can talk. "Does everything have to be a joke, Buck?"

"Mom, can I ..."

"Buck, can this wait? Your dad and I have had a really long day. Miss DeJesus brought her kids in for a cleaning. The girl is great, but those twins!"

"But can I? ..."

"Buck, I'm starved. By the way, nice make-up. Really brings out your eyes. I'm not too crazy about the lipstick, though."

"But, Dad ..."

"Okay, what is it, Buck?" he asks while blowing his breathe. He always does that when I try to talk to him, like he's got somewhere more important he has to be.

"Um ... well ... can I have a drink of water?"

"The word is MAY, not CAN, Buck. Let me untie you so you can stop acting so silly. Nothing is ever serious with you, is it? And take a shower, boy, you stink!"

The story of my life. *Sigh* ... Any of you want to buy a family? Cheap! Real cheap!!!

13

I AM LEGENDARY

— *by Dexter Diaz*

Dex

I rode my bike up the driveway and placed it on the hooks on the wall of the garage. Then I went into the house through the door that connects the garage to the kitchen. The one thing that is always there to greet me is the smell of something cooking. Sometimes it's my mom's cooking, sometimes it's my aunt's, but most times it's my grandmother's.

"Hola, Abuela," I say to my grandmother.

"*Ah, hola, mi corazon!**" she says touching her heart as she looks at me. Then she gently touches my face before hugging me like she hasn't seen me in years. I like that. She lives upstairs, but most times she's down here making breakfast or dinner. The only times she's usually up in her room is to sleep or to watch her *novellas* on TV. They're like Spanish soap operas. When those are on she wants to be alone *'cause* she doesn't want anyone disturbing her. I tried watching them once or twice — not my thing.

"*Quítate los anteojos por favor,***" she says as she points to her eyes. I take off my sunglasses and put them on the table near the door so I don't forget them in the morning. She doesn't speak much English, so I won't bore you by translating our whole conversation. I grab a *Malta* from the fridge and sit at the table to wait for everyone else to come. My mom enters the room next. Today she went to help out at my dad's shop *'cause* I guess his receptionist is sick. Most times she just goes in every few weeks to do bookkeeping and pay the bills. She's really good with money. And even though she's older now, she's still pretty, so I think Papi′ likes to show her off to the customers. Like he's saying, "Look who I married!" *Yo*, there's a picture of my mom and dad when they got married and she looks just like J-Lo, I swear!

She asks me how my day was, I tell her. All the while I hear my sister Christina singing in her room. I wish her walls were soundproof. The door from the downstairs opens and out come Titi (my mom's sister) and her son Christian (he's the one we call Papito. Remember? I told you about him). He takes a seat next to me and asks if he can have a sip of my Malta. I let him. Titi washes her hands so she can help my mom and Abuela with dinner. It's funny, Papito looks up to me, but I'd give anything to trade places with him. Everyone goes crazy over him *'cause* he's got sandy blonde hair and blue eyes! He looks like a little Puerto Rican Bratt Pitt!

Christina comes in the kitchen to help serve dinner. The last one to come to the table is my dad. He's always the last. He sits down and within seconds, the table is full of food. He looks at each of us and smiles.

---

* "Ah, hello my heart!" **94** ** "Take off your glasses, please."

"*Hola, mi esposa*," he says as he blows a kiss to my mother, *Machito* (that's me), *mi' ja* (short for 'mi hija' which means 'my daughter.'), *Papito* (Christian), Carmen (that's Titi), y mi *hermosa madre*!" (That means "my beautiful mother.") Then Papi´ (my dad) says grace and we all start to eat. I really wish that I could just grab dinner and take it up to my room, but my family would never stand for that. Dinner is really important in this house. My dad isn't even done working today, but he comes home just so we can eat together as a family. When he's done, most times he goes back to the shop so he can have his customers' cars ready in case they want to pick them up first thing in the morning.

When we're outside the house, we pretty much eat what everyone else eats. But my grandmother is *ol' school*, so she always makes us traditional Spanish dishes. Meaning we still eat the same way that she did when she was growing up in Puerto Rico. Lots of rice and beans, plantanos, lots of chicken … man, I love Abuela's cooking!!!

But even though we're all family, you'd never know it just by looking at us. Abuela and my dad are really dark skinned. Shoot, they're darker than most African Americans. Then there's my mom and Titi who are pretty light. My sister is like them, too. I'm darker than them, but not nearly as dark as Dad. And finally there's little Brad Pitt who looks like he should be part of some family in Beverly Hills or something. If you saw him, you'd never think he was Puerto Rican. 'sta loca! And to be honest, with the way everyone treats him sometimes, it's like they don't want him to know that he is. It must be so cool to be in a white family where they don't compare their skin color. Not that I want to be like that, I like being Puerto Rican, I just don't like the whole color thing, that's all.

For the next hour we eat dinner and talk. "How was your day?" "*Bien*, how was your day?" We eat some more, "And how was your day?" Okay, everyone's day was *bien*, so can I go now? My principal is from another planet!

While the adults are having coffee, I ask if I can be excused. Luckily they say yes. I thank my grandmother for dinner, grab a coconut soda from the fridge (I'm really thirsty), snatch a shortbread cookie off my sister's plate, ignore her yelling at me, and head up to my room.

Now I had to figure out what to do about my problem. If I was *gonna* have to spend the rest of my life fighting off aliens, then I needed my skills to be sharp. So I spent the rest of the night playing some of my Halo games.

On *legendary mode!* That's the hardest level there is! I know some of them are *kinda* old, but they're still my favorites. I squashed alien after alien. *Plasma Pistol, Needler,* a few *Frag Grenades …* I was *ownin'* those aliens, *bro!* Next thing I know, it was after midnight. *Oops!* I really got carried away. That's enough for tonight. I go to the bathroom and stick my head under the faucet to get a drink of water. A nice long drink.

Guess I'll have to worry about fighting off an alien invasion when the time comes. Right now, I'm *gettin'* sleepy. I take off my sweatshirt and hang it on the doorknob of my closet. I put my pants by the side of the bed. I'll sleep in my t-shirt and boxers.

Bring on the alien invasion, I'll be ready for you. Only thing is, if I have to fight off Martians in real life, how do I get ahold of a real-life *Plasma Pistol?*

14
I REALLY AM FULL OF BOLOGNA
— by Kimmy Kampbell

Kimmy

My mom and I spend a lot of time in this park. I used to come here with my daddy too. But it was different. Mom takes the blanket from the back and spreads it over our usual spot overlooking the lake. Some people call it a pond.

She takes out the newspaper and starts looking through the classified section. That's where you look when you need a job. I keep telling her to look online, but she's kind of old fashioned when it comes to that.

"Can we go to the library later so I can use my computer, Mom?"

"No, not today, Kimmy."

"But I need Wi-Fi so I can write my blog."

"Tomorrow, Kimmy, I promise. Now, aren't you going to eat your sandwich?"

"Frowny face! I'm getting sick of bologna, Mom. Can we get something different next time? Like corned beef or honey-roasted turkey?"

"We'll see, honey, but the new sales won't start until Saturday. Now eat your sandwich so you can start your homework while it's still light out. There are a couple of bottles of water behind the seat."

"sigh … *kk*." For some strange reason, that Buck kid popped into my mind and I picture him saying something stupid like, "Hey, Kimmy, you really are *full of bologna!*" I imagine myself punching him in the arm and he cries out in pain. That makes me smile.

"What's funny, sweetie?"

"Oh, nothing, Mommy. Just thinking about a boy from school."

"Oh, really? Who's the lucky guy?"

"Oh, *ewww*, don't even! It's not like that at all. I don't like Buck one bit!"

"Relax, Kimmy. I just thought …"

"Well you just thought wrong," I said.

We ate our sandwiches and drank our water. I actually had two bottles. I was really thirsty. It really hit the spot. Then we sat for a while and talked some more. "I'm still hungry, Mommy," I said. "Do we have any snacks?"

"Oh, Kimmy, I don't think we have any snacks. Did you bring home anything from school?"

"Yes!" I said excitedly. "I brought us a couple of yogurts, and a few apples. Would you like one?"

"*Mmmm*, I'd love a yogurt, Kimmy. Thank you."

"No prob, even brought a few plastic spoons."

"You think of everything."

We ate our yogurt and talked for a little while longer. It was *kinda* nice. Like it was before Daddy left.

"Can we buy some snacks tomorrow?"

"Kimmy, please! You know it's ..."

"I know, 'Not in our budget!' Nothings *ever* in our budget anymore!"

Well, *that* sure ruined the mood!

 56 PERCENT OF STUDENTS HAVE PERSONALLY WITNESSED SOME TYPE OF BULLYING AT SCHOOL. — DoSomething.org

15
MY DAY GETS EVEN WORSE!
— by Bobby Bonderman

My dog Sonic is always the first to greet me when I get off the bus. I roll my soccer ball towards him. He always likes that. We usually play in the front yard a bit. My little sister Blossom is usually right behind him. Once she sees me, she cries 'til mom lets her out the door so she can play with me and Sonic. After the day I had, I could use a normal day at home. Blossom's like me, she's adopted too. Now SHE'S the one who's Chinese. So's my other sister Emily. I mean the adopted part, not the Chinese part. She's Japanese. The only one who isn't adopted is my big brother, Bryce. Mr. Popular. And he hates us! So with all the nationalities in my house, I guess it was only a matter of time before I met a real-live Martian. Shoot, I'm just surprised my folks haven't already adopted one.

All of a sudden, I hear my mom yell something at me in Korean! I always forget what it means.

Ugh! With all the Martian stuff going on, I completely forgot … today is KOREAN DAY! Ughhhhhh! …

"Come on, *Boobie*, today's your special day."

Between you and me, I really hate it when she calls me *Boobie*, but if I ever told her not to, she'd collapse in tears. That's why I even *kinda* freaked out when Buck called me that earlier. My mom's got a nickname for all of us. I think the only people in the world who go by more nicknames than us are rappers. But at least *their* names are cool!

"Okay, Mom," I say as I hold the door open for Blossom and Sonic. I walk in slowly, knowing that she definitely has something planned for Korean Day. Something painful and embarrassing. I look up and yep, I nailed it.

"What do you think, *Boobie*? It's a traditional Korean costume called a *Hanbok* (HAN - BO)."

Sighhhh … there was my mom, in a long dress or robe or something, with lots of colors and designs. It would probably look nice if we were in Korea now, or if we were at a special ceremony. Or if it was on someone else besides my mom!

"What do you think?" she asks again.

"Oh … nice, Mom."

"Pretty!" says Blossom.

"Come on, I can't wait for you to see what I cooked."

"Okay, Mom." PLEASE not *kimchi*. Please not *kimchi*. Please … My stomach starts bubbling just at the thought of it. I put my backpack in its spot. We each have our own space where we have to put our stuff. We HAVE to! I put my soccer ball in its place, too.

"Oh, will you look at this?! — Bryce, come down here right now, young man," Mom says while tugging her hair. She does that when she's upset.

A few minutes later, Bryce comes walking down the stairs in slow motion. Huffing and puffing and rolling his eyes up into his big head so far back that he could probably see his brain. If he had one. He stops in front of Mom, but never looks directly at her. Almost as if he's looking at the sun. Mom points at his book bag and stinky sneakers. Bryce sighs, then picks them both up and tosses them where they're supposed to go. His head flips from side to side slowly like his neck is too weak to support it. And you know what? This happens EVERY SINGLE DAY!

My house runs like a clock. We eat, talk about our day, ask to be excused, do our homework, then get an hour to ourselves before it's time to start our bedtime rituals. Blossom gets read her favorite book (*Please Don't Yell at We!*) and a kiss. Emily gets her hair combed and a kiss. I get tucked in, and a kiss. Then I read for a few minutes.

Now I'm reading *"Alvin Ho: Allergic to Dead Bodies, Funerals, and Other Fatal Circumstances."* I read the first three when I was younger, so it's kind of a tradition. Alvin's Asian, and as you know, so am I. So whenever my birthday comes, people always think they have to give me a bunch of Asian stuff. Let's see, I've been given an old Hideki Matsui Yankees poster; a Jeremy Lin basketball jersey; a DVD of Bruce Lee's Enter The Dragon; and a ton of Manga books. I could have really done without the Jackie Chan action figure, though. Luckily I really like the *Alvin Ho* books so I never mind getting those.

Anyway, back to our bedtime ritual: Bryce usually gets a stern talking to. Not sure about the kiss. But probably not. As usual, my dad doesn't come home until after most of us are asleep. There's really not much more to it than that. Even on a day when I find out my principal is from another planet. Pretty boring, huh?

But back to dinner, I wish I could skip it, but I'm not that lucky. You really need to know what goes on in my house. First, Mom puts Blossom's booster seat in one of the chairs and the rest of us sit around the table. And do you know how we know exactly where to sit? Of course you don't. We know *exactly* where to sit because of our dumb placemats.

And do you know what is on the placemats? Flags from where we're from. So mine has the flag of Korea, Blossom's has the Chinese flag, and Emily's is Japanese. Meanwhile Mom has the American flag. Dad, during the few times that he actually eats with us, refuses to use a placemat. So does Bryce. Mom used to give Bryce one, but he kept replacing it with stuff that made her mad. Like once he made his own with a bunch of skulls. He called it his *re-placemat*. I can't say that I blame him either.

Now comes mom's lecture. "The first thing you'll notice is that we'll be using silver chopsticks. I just got them off of *eBay!* I was praying that they'd arrive in time for today's celebration. They're silver because silver changes color if it touches poison."

"You mean there's poison in the food?" yelled Emily.

"Yeah, but only in one portion. Mom and Dad decided that having three of you foreign brats is too much!" snorts Bryce.

"*Brycie*, you stop that right now! That's not funny! Not funny at all!" she snaps at him while tugging her hair.

"Stop calling me *Brycie!* I'm 16!"

Then Mom looks at Emily and says, "There is nothing wrong with your food, *Bunny*. You see, back in ancient Korea, their rulers used them to make sure that their food was safe to eat."

"I wish my food WAS poisoned!" whispers Bryce under his breath. I wish it was, too, I think to myself.

"Now as you'll also see, we will be eating out of bowls instead of plates. I don't know why that is, I just know we're supposed to. Now each bowl has something different in it. See? Rice, cold noodles … and that one is called *Bulgogi**.

"*Ewww!* Sounds gross," says my wonderful big brother. What a great role model he is.

"Manners, Brycie! Anyway, *Bulgogi* is thin slices of beef that I have marinated in soy sauce, sesame oil, garlic and pepper. Now watch how I'm going to take a slice of the beef and wrap it in a lettuce leaf before I eat it."

We watch. Except for Bryce who takes out his phone and starts texting a friend. How he even has *any* friends is beyond me, but hey.

* You probably know what to do by now, right?   **103**

Mom continues her demonstration. Man, it's a good thing we aren't starving, we'd be dead by now. "See? Meat and veggies in one bite. And that is *kimchi*, which is pickled Chinese cabbage. But be careful, it's a little spicy."

And a LOT nasty, I thought to myself.

"But isn't this Korean day?" asks Bryce without looking up from his phone.

"Why, yes it is, Bryce. Excellent question."

"Then why did you make Chinese cabbage? Shouldn't you make that for Emily on Chinese day?" he added.

"I'm Japanese," said Emily, "Blossom is the one who is Chinese."

"Whatever," he snapped. "Just answer the question."

"Well I … I don't know, I'll have to research it some more. But what I DO know is that this is one of the national dishes of Korea."

"Then why don't they use Korean cabbage?"

"Well I … I mean … well, I don't know. I'm sorry, Brycie. I just followed the recipe. Please don't be upset."

"I guess I'll get over it, Mom. Are those pancakes?"

"Yes, bean pancakes."

"Bean? I'm *outta* here before all the farting begins!" Then Brycie gets up, goes to the bread box, grabs a bagel, gets a knife from the drawer and a jar of peanut butter from the cabinet.

"Can I be excused?" he says as he leaves the kitchen not waiting for an answer.

"But don't you want to try these special Korean dishes, Brycie? I made them special for your brother."

"Then make HIM eat it," he says all grumpy, "and he's *not* my brother! None of these little freaks are!"

"BRYCE!" screams Mom. "Just wait 'til your father gets home!"

"When is that, Mom? Midnight again?" he says while leaving the kitchen.

Ouch! Well he's *not* getting any of my bean pancakes now …

Mom stares at him as he walks away. Her eyes burning with anger.

Or sadness. All I know is they're burning. She grabs her napkin from the table, wipes the corner of her eyes, then turns to us and forces her face to smile while tugging her hair again. She's *gonna* be bald one day.

"Okay everyone, napkins on your laps and elbows off the table," said Mom. "Let's all try the *kimchi*."

"*Wahhhhhh!*" That's Blossom starting to cry. I can't say I blame her either.

"Oh, baby, what's wrong?" asks my mom.

"*Don' yike chimchi. Don' wanna* eat," whines my baby sister.

"Aw, c'mon, precious. Look, watch Mommy try it," she says as she grabs the chopsticks off the table. They're silver, you know. Slowly, and carefully, she places the first chopstick on the knuckle of her right hand. Then she picks up the second one and places that between the tips of her index finger and her thumb. The first one falls to the floor.

"Oh, dear!" she says. For my mom, that's pretty foul language. She picks it up off the floor and goes to wash it off.

"Five-second rule," I say to her.

"Not in this house, Bobby. Germs are not something to be taken lightly!"

She sits down and tries it again. The chopstick hits the floor again. She gets up and washes it off again.

After the third time, she gets us all forks. Thank goodness!

"Okay, now, Blossom, watch Mommy eat the yummy *kimchi*," she says through a forced smile. She scoops it up, and puts a heaping forkful in her mouth. Her expression changes. That means even *she* doesn't think it's good. No more smile.

"Pretty good, huh, Mom?" I say with my lip quivering trying not to laugh.

"Well, it's … interesting," she says.

"Then have some more! Set a good example for us, Mom." Now I'm *really* trying not to laugh. I drink a glass of water to try to calm down.

"Well, kids, I'm thinking that maybe something didn't turn out quite right with Mommy's recipe. Maybe we should skip the *kimchi* and just eat the other things. And when you're done, you can have some of Mommy's rice cookies for dessert."

"And can I have some ice cream too, Mom?"

"*Hmmm* … well okay, Boobie, but only *one* scoop."

Man! See what I mean? It's like I asked her for a kidney!

"Cookies!" Blossom yells.

"Do you think we should take some cookies to your brother?" Mom asks. "He seemed so upset, maybe he could use a treat."

"Don't worry, about him, Mom," I said, "Bryce has so much junk food in his closet that he could open up a candy store."

"What?!!!" she screamed like someone just kicked her in the shin. "You mean, he's hiding sweets in his room? Well I'm going to put a stop to that right now!" she says as she stomps up the stairs.

Oops!

And that's how our Asian celebrations go in my house. Korean Day for me, Chinese Day for Blossom, Japanese Day for Emily and Jerk Day for Bryce. I'll bet you guys are pretty jealous, huh?

"Look at all this junk!" I hear my mom yell from Bryce's room. "Wait 'til I tell your father!"

"Whatever!" I'll bet you can guess who said *that*.

After she cools down, she'll come back downstairs and put on some Korean music to bring me closer to my heritage … well at least for another month.

I can't wait for her to dress up like a Ninja for Emily's day!

106

GOING TO SLEEP

— *by Mina Madsen*

I can't believe my principal is a Martian. What am I going to do now? I can't tell my parents, they'll think this is another story that I'm making up just to get attention. And forget about Joy. We don't talk about anything. So I definitely won't waste my time talking to her about *this!* Knowing her, she'll probably go and tell Daddy anyway.

I finish putting on my pajamas then brush my teeth. I drink another cup of water. That's like the 40th one tonight. Joy knocks on the door for me to hurry up. She does that every night. I ignore her. I do *that* every night. I open the door and walk right past her like she doesn't exist.

"Good night, Mina," she sings in a voice that's so sweet that it makes me *wanna* gag. I walk down the hall and open the door to my room. Put my dirty clothes in the hamper, lift up Chauncey (my Teddy bear), pull back the covers then hop into the bed. *Oops*, almost forgot. I get up and run back to the hamper to take the balled-up napkin out of my pocket. Before I get back into bed, I run down the hall to get another drink of water. I take the necklace out and slip it under my pillow. Then I snuggle up with my Chauncey as I get comfortable.

My principal is a Martian! That thought just kept bouncing around my head over and over. Next thing I know, my clock says 11 p.m. Then 12:15 a.m. And I'm still wide awake, thinking about what school is going to be like for me from now on. And what does he plan to do with us now that we know his secret? Will he be extra nice? Or will we end up being a topping on some kind of Martian salad?

BUENOS NOCHES*
— by Dexter Diaz

Yo, Principal Marshand is a Martian!!!!

'sta loca!

Man! I'm really thirsty, *bro!*

* Check out the meaning in the *"A Little Bit From Dex"* page in the back of the book.

108

BEDTIME

— *by Bobby Bonderman*

It's shower time, which means that I'm sitting on my clothes hamper with the water running while playing Angry Birds. Every couple of minutes I stick my head under the sink to get a drink of water. My body feels like I've been stuck in a desert for months! Must be from my mom's *kimchi*.

Dude, my head of school is from another planet. Finally something exciting. That's the coolest thing that's *ever* happened to me, unless he decides to eat me. Which would not be so cool. Maybe when he goes back to Mars I can pay him to take Bryce along.

HITTIN' THE SACK

— *by Buck Bievers*

Dag! My principal is an alien ... hey that explains why he never laughs at my jokes. Maybe they don't have comedy on Mars! Maybe I can get him to take my sisters back with him!!!

I can't believe I wet my pants!!!

NIGHTY NIGHT

— by Kimmy Kampbell

"Nighty night, honey, don't let the bed bugs bite," says my mom as she hands me a blanket. I reach down and grab one of the handles of my chair. I pull it until the back of my seat reclines. When it's down as far as it can go, I reach into the backseat of the minivan to get my pillow.

"Good night, Mommy."

"Good night, Kimmy. Mommy loves you."

"Me, too."

"Always have your own bank account, sweetie. Promise me you'll remember that."

"I will, Mommy. I promise."

"And what else do I tell you, Kimmy?"

"That it's okay to *want* a husband when I get older, but don't ever put myself in the position where I *need* a husband."

"Right. Good night, sweetheart."

"Night, Mom." This has been one of the worst days of my life! ... I can't believe Tessa and Samantha said that no one in the school likes me. Those *stringbings* are *gonna* pay. They'll see!

21

HELLO, KITTY!

— by Mina Madsen

Hey! I'm back at school … and on the four-square court. How did I get here? Maybe all that Martian stuff was just a dream. Yeah, that's it, I must have, *like*, dozed off at recess or something. Oh, well, time to play. But when I looked over at the court. No one was there. *Hmmm* … I looked around some more. Still no one. Then finally I look at the wall over by the tether ball court and see what looks like the top of a few heads. So I head in that direction. Maybe they're all hiding from me because they're afraid to play me. Mom always says that, "Fear is a powerful teammate."

As I walk around the wall and turn the corner, I see a bunch of kids kneeling on the ground.

"Hey, what are you losers up to?" I ask.

"SHHHHHHH!" they all say at the same time. Wow, these guys are really freaking out.

"Huh? Will somebody tell me what's going on?" Now I'm getting annoyed.

"Get down before it sees you!" says C. J. And if I didn't know better, I'd swear he was shaking. In fact, they all were. And when I got a better look at them, they were, *like,* all-bruised up and stuff. Emma looked like she had been hit in the face with a rock. And Nick had another nosebleed.

"Wow, what happened to you guys?" I asked.

"Just, get down, Mina!" shouts Meagan.

"I'm not hiding from anyone!" I say defiantly. "And what do you mean *it?* Is there a wild dog on the loose? Or a bear?"

Just then I heard a noise, like a heavy thumping sound.

"Worse!" says Jenna. "A whole lot worse!"

I hear the thumping get closer, and as it does, it also speeds up. Now, I have to admit, I'm starting to get a little nervous, too!

"Oh, no!" screams Elizabeth, "It found us! It found us!" Then all at once, they turn and look over at the bushes just in time to see something, and I'm not sure what, land in front of them. It's like it just jumped right over the hedges.

"What the heck is that?!" I yell out. It was the scariest thing I've ever seen in my entire life. It was like a big black figure with bright red eyes. And it must have been, *like*, ten-feet tall! I've never felt so small and weak in my

whole life. I backed away slowly, watching to see what it was going to do.

Then everyone screamed. Boys, girls, everyone. Sam was the first one to stand up. "Run!" he said. "It found us!"

Just then, that ... thing ... lifts its arm up and flings something forward. I don't know what it threw, but it was on fire, and it hit Sam square in the back. And *boom!* He was gone. Just like that. It's like he just disintegrated or something.

Now everyone was screaming ... and running. *Boom!* I heard again. This time it was Christopher. Gone in, *like*, a puff of smoke or something. All I know is that it was time for me to go. I kicked off my red flip flops and started running as fast as I could. But I heard the footsteps right on my tail.

Thump! Thump! Thump!

I heard Hannah scream. Then *boom!*

I ran up the stairs from the playground and turned to run into the gym, but the door was locked. I looked back at that thing only to see it throw one of those flaming round-things again. I dove to the ground just in time to avoid it. But whoever was standing next to me, wasn't so lucky. By the time I looked over, all that was remaining was a sneaker and a puff of smoke.

I got up to run again.

"Help me, Mina!"

"Yeah, help me, Mina!"

"Me, too!"

I was too nervous to tell who was talking.

Thump! Thump! Thump!

I hid behind one of the cars that was parked in the circle.

Slowly, but surely, all the screaming stopped. As much as I hate all those kids, I'd be so happy right now if one of them was with me right now. Even Jenna. Then, just when I thought I was safe, the heavy footsteps started up again. *Thump! Thump! Thump!* Closer and closer. Then it stopped. I turned around slowly, fearing that it was behind me. But when I looked, there was nothing.

Whew! Maybe I'm safe. Then a sudden noise to my left made me look over my shoulder. All I saw were those two glowing red eyes staring at me.

It lifted its arms and next thing I know I see this big fireball coming right at me. There's nothing I can do. Not even enough time to scream. If this thing wanted to make me scared, it did it!

BOOM!

****

Ahhhh! I turn and fall. But when I land, I'm in my living room. You mean I'm not dead? *Omigosh!* That was, *like*, the worst dream I have ever had in my entire life! That thing was right out of a horror movie. I sit up and wipe my forehead. Wow, I must have been sweating in my sleep, my hand is actually wet. I try to calm myself down by taking deep breaths. After a few minutes, my heart stops pounding and I can feel my body start to relax. But just when I start to feel better, I look around my living room, and notice something really strange. The furniture is gigantic! I'm, *like*, one of those tiny guys from that Gulliver story. It's strange, but *kinda* cool, too.

Then all of a sudden it got dark. I mean, it was already dark, but now it's *really* dark. I can see the clock on the cable box says it's 3:16 a.m. That's the only light coming from in front of me. It's the light behind me that just went out. I wonder what happened? There must be some sort of black out or something. Wait, it didn't go out … there's something blocking it. I turned slowly. It's Hairball, Joy's stupid cat! Joy's *gigantic*, stupid, *hissing* cat! Either he grew to be the size of a building, or I shrunk!

"Nice, kitty." I said. More hissing. So I tried a different approach. "Bad, kitty, go to your room!" More hissing. I backed up slowly, and she kept coming. But now I was up against the wall with no place left to go. I looked to my left and saw a *super ball.* That's one of those tiny little balls that are really really bouncy, Joy must have gotten it in a goodie bag from someone's lame birthday party. Obviously I wasn't invited.

Slowly I reached down and picked it up. It was even bigger than my head. Then I took a deep breath, tossed the ball into the air, and punched it with my fist as hard as I could, just like I was serving in four-square. The ball hit Hairball right between the eyes. She meowed, then turned back in my direction. I ducked as a giant paw swung and barely missed my head. Now it was time to try a third approach.

RUNNING!

I dove out the way as Hairball came crashing down on the spot where I was. Now it was a foot race. And when I tell you I was running fast, I mean I was running, *like*, F-A-S-T. Only bad thing is it's my two tiny little feet trying to outrun her four gigantic paws. No fair! She leaps, I *zig*. She *zigs*. I *zag*. I can't believe how fast I'm running, but it's still not enough to get away from her. Good thing this is a dream, if not I might end up as a chew toy. But since it *is* a dream, let's see what I can do. Might as well have some fun. Okay, imaginary Hairball, let's see how good you are. Besides, I never wanted a cat anyway, you're Joy's mangy ol' feline.

While I'm running, I do a quick look around the room to see what I'm working with. Throw rug ... couch ... coffee table ... *oohhh*, her travel container! That's what they put her in when they take her on trips, and it's just what I need. I *zag* again as Hairball goes flying over my head. *Meowwww!* I run for the couch. I know I can fit underneath without ducking or slowing down, but I'm not so sure about Joy's fat cat. Let's hope not. I make it across the room in about three-seconds-flat. Luckily it takes Hairball about 5 seconds. She tries to hit the brakes as she approaches the couch. I go under, she goes *thump!*

Then, while she runs around to meet me on the other side, I get a headstart running towards the throw rug. Mom has these tiny little rugs all over the house. She keeps talking about how beautiful our wood floor is, then she covers most of it with rugs.

Go figure.

Now it's a straight sprint. Loser gets locked up, or in my case, eaten. I run until I get to the throw rug, then stop short. Hairball leaps. I leap too. But this time I have a plan. She lands on the rug and her weight makes it impossible for her to stop. The rug slides forward. I climb on top of her travel container and pull the door open. She continues to slide forward, right into the container. I jump off the top, grab the door and let my weight pull it shut. She sees the door closing and pulls her paw back just in the nick of time. I climb up and swing the latch closed. Don't see the lock anywhere, but I *do* see a pencil. I run over and grab it, then scale the front of the cage and jam the pencil through the latch holes to keep the door shut.

Now that Hairball is locked safely inside the cage, there's only one thing left to do. "Hey, fatty, guess you're not so fast after all, are you? I guess your precious *wittle* 'Joy Joy' has been giving you too many Tabby Treats, huh? Well it looks like you could stand to shed a few pounds, don't you think?"

Whew! I'm beat. I look around the room. Not too much damage. Just the rug, and a few things that must have gotten knocked over during the chase. I'm not exactly sure when. Then I look over towards the kitchen, and I see the most wonderful sight in the world — a box of Lucky Charms, my favorite cereal of all time! I get a running start, jump and grab onto the leg of one of the dining room chairs. I keep my arms and legs moving until I climb all the way up the back. Then I leap onto the table and jump into the box to knock it over. The box tips over, spilling its marshmallow goodness all over the table like a piñata.

Then I saw my reflection in a glass of water that I must have left here from dinner. Not only am I, *like*, really tiny, but I've got that silly Martian uniform on again. You know, the one I tried on after I touched that glowing thingy. And my hair is different, too. It's black now, instead of blonde, and it's in two big puffs that almost look like I'm wearing a Mickey Mouse hat. Even my nose and mouth are different. And these ears! Boy do I look funny! Thank goodness it's only a dream!

Ugh! Two nightmares in one night! Oh well, time to dig into those Lucky Charms. I'll be sure to leave all the hard brown parts for Joy. She'll hate that!

So at least *this* dream ends happily.

22

POSTING ON MY WALL

— *by Kimmy*

Some people remember the dreams they have at night, but not me. I almost never do. Which is good, 'cause most of the ones I hear about are pretty stupid anyway. Like the one I'm having now. It's all white, everywhere I look, except for this gigantic wall in front of me. It's white, too, except for a blue stripe across the top. No wonder I don't remember my dreams, they're boring!

Then all of a sudden, something started to happen to the wall. It started moving. Not the whole thing, just in the middle. Hey, it looks like the letter "K." Next was an "I." I'll bet it's spelling my name. Well, why not, it is *my* dream! I was right, it did spell my name. But it didn't stop, it added another "I" and then another letter. "Kimmy is …" it says so far. Now another "S" and a "T." I'll bet it's *gonna* say "stupendous!"

But it didn't! "Kimmy is stupid! Hey, who wrote that?!"

I heard someone laugh and immediately turned around to see who I was about to put in their place. But there wasn't anyone there. And when I turned back to look at the wall, there was something else posted on it.

"Kimmy is a cow!"

"Really?!" I said out loud. More laughter. Still no one around to pound.

Then another one appeared that said, "Kimmy has a big mouth." And another, "Kimmy's clothes are cheap."

WHAT?! Now whoever it is has gone too far. No one talks about my clothes! One by one, these insults appeared. And the more there were, the more laughing there was. I tried to cover up some of the words, but they were much too big. There I was, standing in front of a huge wall of insults, and there was nothing that I could do.

"If you ask me," I started yelling at the top of my lungs, "You're a coward! *Anyone* can write bad stuff about people if they're not there to see it. Why don't you say it to my face instead?! … Because you know it's not true, that's why, plus you're a chicken! You're one big fat chicken!"

What kind of person does that kind of thing anyway?

119

I woke up swinging my arms in anger. Mom was still sound asleep. The moon was really bright so I went to cover my eyes with my hand. But nothing happened. I mean, I lifted my arm, put my hand over my face, but there was no shade. Then when I turned my hand at a different angle, I saw why. I was *flat!!! OMG!* And I don't mean flat like … um … name something that's flat … like a book, I mean *flat-as-a-piece-of-paper-flat!* Not just my arm either, all of me!!! I didn't know what to do. Was I still dreaming? What if I'm not? Should I wake up my mom? If it's scaring *me*, it might give *her* a heart attack!!! My mom is not like me, she can be *very* dramatic!

After about 10 minutes or so, I finally stopped shaking. Well almost. I looked at myself and not only was I flat, but I was in that Martian uniform again. You know, the one I tried on in the Principal's lab? Then I looked at the window, we always keep it cracked just a little so the fresh air can get in while we sleep, but not big enough for a bat or something to fly through. For some reason I climbed up on my chair then lifted up my leg and put it through the window and gently slid down. I made it through without a problem. I leaned over to look at myself in the side mirror. Hey, my hair is different. Really different. Instead of my beautiful long red French braid, my hair is black and wavy. And it kinda swishes over my face covering my right eye. Actually, it's quite fashionable. My lips are different, too. They're fuller. Like I got a *collagen shot* from one of those fancy plastic surgeons that you see on TV. I really like the way they look, so I stare in the side mirror and make kissy-faces.

Next I decided to walk around the park. Every once in a while a gust of wind would come by and I thought it would lift me up in the air a few inches like a kite, but it didn't. I guess even though I was flat, maybe I stayed the same weight. Just my luck, I'm flat as a pancake but still a porker. Do you know what it's like to be the biggest kid in your whole grade ever since kindergarten? Both in height *and* weight. Thank goodness some of the boys are finally starting to catch up to me so I don't get called a lot of the names that I used to get called in lower school. Like "giant" or "Hulk Girl."

After a while, it hit me, I was so freaked out about being flat that I didn't even realize that I was walking alone in the park. I'd never do that at night in real life. Then all of a sudden, I got a little scared. Strange noises. The *eerie* light of the moon. Plus there was so much stuff moving around. But once I saw a raccoon, I knew it was time to get back to the van. Dream or no dream, I hear those things can be vicious! I made my way back to the minivan, then climbed through the window and sat down. My heart was beating a thousand times a minute. I know I always wanted to be thin, but this is ridiculous!!! I concentrated real hard to see if I could make myself normal again. Focus focus focus ... then poof. Back to my normal size ... and in my regular clothes again. *Whew!*

To make this dream even weirder, all of our water bottles are empty. Mom would freak out if she saw this 'cause she just bought them. She'd probably make us drink out of the pond until they went on sale again. They say that your dreams have meanings. If so, I wonder what this one means? I hope I remember this when I wake up.

Maybe I'll even blog about the last dream when I was thin. But I definitely won't tell anyone about the stupid writing-on-the-wall dream.

23
YOU CAN'T HANDLE THE TOOTH!
— by Buck Bievers

Here I am, back in line in the cafeteria. Boy, it seems like everytime I turn around, I'm here. This must be how Kimmy feels.

"Hey, look everyone, it's Buck Pee-vers, the kid who peed on himself," I heard a voice say from behind me followed by laughter.

"How did you know that?!" I exclaimed. "I mean, no I didn't, you must have me confused with someone else."

"When you're with Buck, URINE (you're in) good hands," says someone else. More laughter. I spun around to see who said it, but didn't see anyone.

"Who said that?" I demanded.

Not a sound. The insults continued, "Hey, I thought Buck was African American, but now we all know he's Euro-Peein'!"

I look up to see milk shooting through four giant noses that are floating in the air above me. If I'm not dreaming then I've lost my mind.

"That's not funny!*" I said. Did I really just say, "That's not funny"? Where are my witty comebacks? I can't think of anything to say.

"How does Buck listen to music?" another voice asked. I turned around to see him before he gave the punchline. But I still didn't see anyone. "On an M-PEE-3 player!" said a voice. More laughter, and more milk gushers. Man! Whichever way I turn, the voice is always behind me! And the milk keeps rising. It's over my ankles now.

"Hey, who's Buck's favorite rapper?" … "PEE-Diddy!"

"Buck's favorite line from Shakespeare is 'to PEE or not to Pee.'"

The more they laughed, the more milk gushed. It rose past my knees, over my stomach, and kept getting higher. More jokes. More laughs. More milk! Finally it was so high that I had to stand on my tip-toes to breathe. *Dag!* I *really* should have taken those swimming lessons in camp! Next thing I knew, the milk rose over my head and I was splashing around like … well, like someone who's about to drown. Boy, talk about crying over spilled milk! I went under and everything went black.

Then it got light again. I finally woke up! *Whew!*

The clock said 2 a.m. But apparently the weirdness of my nightmare wasn't over. I felt something sticking out of my mouth. I reached with my hand and I was right. There IS something coming out of my mouth. I started to freak out. I grabbed it and tried to yank it out, but whatever it was, was

*Ha ha, made you look!   **123**

Buck

really sharp, so I snatched my hand away quickly.

I started to freak out so I hopped out the bed and tip-toed down to the bathroom taking extra care not to wake up anyone, especially not my *three-big-mouthed-evil-sisters*. And when I stared into the mirror … I looked like a metal sabre-tooth tiger!!! My teeth are like six inches long and they look like knives. I can't get over my hair either. It looks like I have a bunch of Kimmy's red braids!!! And I don't mean like her normal shade of red, I mean like red-paint red. Where the heck did this come from? This is the freakiest nightmare ever!!! Even my nose was different. If I didn't know better, I'd swear I was looking at a total stranger. Plus I was in those Martian clothes again. Although I *hafta* admit, that was the coolest part of my appearance. I look like Superman. But then I felt that warm feeling on my legs again. Aw, man! Stupid weak bladder. But the weird thing is that the warm feeling seemed to go away after a few seconds. I guess this uniform is super absorbent!

I couldn't help but look at myself in the mirror. I kept waiting for something else to happen. You know, like being attacked by a monster or something. But nothing did. Finally I just got back in my bed. Hey, that's *kinda* funny. Having a dream about going back to sleep. I had to lay on my back to keep from ripping up my pillows with these teeth.

I didn't remember a whole lot when I woke up in the morning. I was just happy that my teeth were back to normal and I was even back in my Bart Simpson pajamas. Although I wouldn't mind having a real costume like that. That would be the *sickest* Halloween costume ever!

 APPROXIMATELY 160,000 TEENS SKIP SCHOOL EVERY DAY BECAUSE OF BULLYING. — DoSomething.org

24
RISE 'N' WHINE
— *by Mina Madsen*

My alarm went off about 10 minutes ago. But instead of getting up, I rolled over to try to get five more minutes. I usually let Joy get into the bathroom first. But instead of going back to sleep, something just popped into my head that woke me right up. I had the weirdest dreams ever last night. Not sure which was worse, running from that giant shadow creature with the red eyes and flaming rocks, or almost being eaten by Joy's stupid cat! Usually I can't wait for the day to be over, this time I couldn't wait for the night to be over. I tried to remember it all before it started to fade.

Joy is finally done in the bathroom and from the sound of it, she's heading downstairs. I guess it's time to drag myself *outta* bed.

"Mom! Mom!" she screams.

"What is it, Joy?"

"Oh what is that crazy girl complaining about now?" I say out loud.

"Come look what Mina did! She locked Snowball in her kennel all night!"

Wait, what did she say, I did what? "I didn't touch Hairball, Mom, I've been in bed all night!"

"For the last time, Mina, her name is Snowball, not Hairball! And look, she locked her in her cage and jammed a pencil in the lock!"

I heard Mom go downstairs. "Mina! Did you pour cereal all over my table?"

"And look, Mommy, she ate all the *Charms* out of the cereal, all that's left is the *Lucky!* She knows I hate that!"

"MINA!!!"

Uh-oh. I think to myself.

25

THE NEXT DAY

— *by Buck Bievers*

When the school bus pulled up at Bobby's house, I couldn't wait to talk to him. I even saved him a seat. As soon as he got on, he started looking around. When he saw me, his eyes opened up wider — mine probably did too — and he started walking towards the back.

"'sup?" I said as he sat down next to me.

"What's up?" he said back.

And that was it. I thought we'd talk the whole bus ride about what happened. But neither of us said a word. And for me *not* to talk, you know something is wrong.

Sigh! ... This is one time that I wish we were girls. They can talk about anything. It's always okay for them to share their feelings. Why not us?

I took out my sketchbook and started to draw how I looked in my dream. The big teeth. The long red braids. I didn't show Bobby though. I won't show anyone.

When the bus pulled up to school, we both got off and walked around the circle to the middle school building. We gave each other a nod then split up when we got to the entrance.

26
IHOP, UHOP, WE ALL HOP FOR PANCAKES!
— *by Kimmy Kampbell*

Kimmy

When I woke up a few hours later, the first thing I did was look at my arm. Nope, not paper-thin. *Whew!* I know it sounds silly, but my dream seemed so real that I just wanted to check to make sure. Mom and I started our day by driving to IHOP. We only do it every once in a while, so it's always a treat. Most times, we just have bagels or donuts or something. Especially if Mom finds a good batch in the day-old section. We got our vanity bags out of the trunk, went inside and had the waitress show us to a table. While our food was being cooked, we went to the ladies room, washed up, changed our clothes and brushed our teeth. We try to do it as quickly as possible so we don't get caught.

I really wanted to order the *Rooty Tooty Fresh 'N Fruity,* but I didn't want to hear Mom talk about our budget, so I just got a small stack of strawberry banana pancakes. After we ate, Mom paid our bill in cash, since she doesn't have credit cards anymore, then drove me to school.

"Mom?" I asked.

"Yes, sweetie?"

"Can we go to the storage place soon? I need to get my summer shoes. My feet get really hot in these boots."

"Sure, sweetie, I keep meaning to, but I get distracted. And remind me if you still want to go to the library today to use their Wi-Fi."

"Thanks, Mommy."

We talked a bit as she drove me to school. She knows to let me out in the back parking lot, which she did. When I got out, I turned to wave. She blew me a kiss, the way she always does. I don't mind it so much when we're back here where no one can see us.

"Bye, Mommy."

"Bye, sweetie," she said. "Oh, and Kimmy? ..."

"Yes, Mommy?"

"Say hi to Buck for me!" she said while making kissy noises! Then she drove off before I had a chance to respond.

"I'll get you for that!!!" I said laughing. Sometimes I forget how funny she can be.

27

I FORGIVE YOU, MI'JO
— *by Dexter Diaz*

Dex

I woke up to the sounds of the usual noise in my house. My dad getting ready to go to the shop. My mom already getting started with the house work. Abuela's cane hitting each step on her way down to make us all breakfast. And of course, my sister singing as she does her hair in the bathroom.

I wipe the gunk *outta* my eyes and spin around to get out of bed. But when my feet touched the floor, it felt like I was stepping on a pile of stuff. There were books everywhere. It looked like someone took every book in the house and dumped it by the side of my bed. Even the old encyclopedias that are too ancient to use, but for some reason, we never get rid of. They're from, like, 1976 or something. I keep telling my folks that I can get all the info I need from Google, but they insist that these old brown books are the way to go. I don't think they really trust the Internet. I step over the books so I can get the pants that I wore yesterday. I like them *'cause* they're really comfortable, plus all my stuff is already in the pockets. Besides, I could wear these pants every day until I graduate and no one is going to say anything to me. Not if they know what's good for them! Who would have put all these books in my room? My sister? *Nah!* ... Is it my Dad's way of telling me that I should read more? Well, it doesn't *seem* like something he'd do. Ricky Martin? No, he idolizes me. But who else in the house would do it? *Hmmmm. 'sta loco!* REALLY LOCO.

I wait for my sister to leave the bathroom to get something out of her room, then I rush in and lock the door behind me.

By the time she comes back and starts to bang on the door like a crazy woman, I'm already done washing up. I open the door and stare at her in case she wants to mention anything about the books.

"What?" she says, as she rushes past me and slams the door.

Man, I just *wanna* get to school today. I know, that's *loco* coming from me, right? But I just *wanna* talk to the other guys to see what's up. I mean, what are we *gonna* do about this whole Martian thing? But my house is *not* the *kinda* house where I can just grab a Pop-Tart and run out. *Uh-uh.* In my house, we have a full hot breakfast EVERY SINGLE MORNING! I know I shouldn't complain. Guess it beats some of the crappy cereals that you guys have to eat. And I'm not just talking about common stuff like eggs either. Abuela likes to make *Maizena** which is like a sweet custard. Man, it's actually good enough to have for dessert, but we have it for breakfast. Plus there's usually lots of juice, fresh fruit (Abuela would rather die than eat fruit from a can!), eggs, some *kinda* meat and, of course, plantains. Plus lots of coffee. I pass on that, but my sister has it sometimes. I think it makes her feel grown. Show off.

As I make it downstairs, I see my dad sitting at the table. He smiles when he sees me. Not his usual really happy smile that lights up his face. But one like it *kinda* hurt to do it. He stood up and waved for me to follow him to the garage.

My mom comes in and asks, "Dexter, do you know what happened to the encyclopedias? And the books from the shelf in the den are gone, too.

"Oh, si, Mami´, they're in my room. I'll … uh … put them back when I get home. I was looking for some information."

"Oh, *bien*. See, I knew we shouldn't have thrown those out," she said. "Breakfast will be ready soon."

"Hey, Dexter, look at me!" yells Papito as he starts to bang on the conga drums like he's having a seizure.

"Oh, you are soooo good," says my mom while clapping. "You're going to be the next Ray Barretto!"

"Ah, si! Ray Barretto!" says Abuela peeking her head in from the kitchen.

He made a record way back that became the first Latin song to be on the Billboard charts. That was a big deal back then. I'm talking about Ray Barretto, not Papito.

I looked back at my dad who began to head towards the garage. I decided to skip the rest of the concert and went in after him and closed the door. After a few seconds, he began to talk.

"Machito, I know how much you say you hate school."

I opened my mouth to interrupt, but he put his hand up, so I shut up.

"Although, I have to say that I'm happy that you took those books up to your room. I hope this means that you're going to try harder. I also know that you want to work in my shop. But that's not what I want for you. I want you to be better. I want you to do more than I did. Now don't get me wrong. I think I've done okay for myself. Better than *my* father. But I don't want you working with your hands all day. It's hard work. I want you to work with your brain … so I'm giving you my blessings."

"Um … blessings for what, Papi´?"

"I'm giving you my permission … my permission … to be better than me!"

What do you say to something like that? Thanks? No thanks? I didn't *wanna* crack a joke, because whatever he was talking about, it was really serious to him. I've never seen him like this.

"Machito, I give you my permission to be a better man than your Papi´." Okay, you may not think this is a big deal, but let me tell you something. In our culture, it's a *very* big deal. Esta *grande!!!*

Wow. I still didn't know what to say, so I just looked at him.

"Did I ever tell you why I didn't really speak to my father?"

"No, not really," I answered. "I heard you and Titi talk about it once, but when I came into the room, you guys stopped. So I never thought I could ask."

"*Umm*, well, up to now, you probably couldn't have. You see, my dad came to this country with almost nothing. He came to this town because his older brother had come here about six months before and promised that he could get him a job in the auto shop where he worked."

"Wait a minute," I interrupted. "You mean he came all the way to the U.S. to work as a mechanic?"

"Don't be disrespectful, Machito. People were very poor in our home in Puerto Rico. Many of the men came here for jobs, then sent the money back home to take care of their families. Then when they had enough money saved, they sent for their wives and kids to join them. So that is what he did. In fact, that's what both he and his brother Ramon did. They worked there for *years!* Never even thought of looking for another job. Puerto Ricans are very loyal. If you're good to us, you're like family. Anyway, back in the 1980s, Mr. Ryan, the owner of Ryan's Auto Repair, where they worked, fell on hard times. His wife had some kind of cancer. He needed money, and lots of it, to try to make her better. Now by that time, me and your Uncle Hector, Ramon's son, had been working in the shop for years, too. Plus we did a lot of stuff on the side. We were always working, he and I. Mowing lawns, landscaping, chopping down trees. And we could fix almost anything. That's where you get it from. So when Mr. Ryan finally had to sell the shop, the two of us had enough money saved to make him an offer."

"Really? Wow, you guys must have been rich."

"Well it turns out that your mother had been saving most of the money that I had been giving her over the years. She started when I would send it to her back in Puerto Rico, and continued once we were here. The same for Hector's wife Zelideth."

"Tia Z?"

"Si. Nobody saves money like those two. I'll bet your mother still has the first dollar I ever gave her. Those two could balance this country's budget in less than a year. Anyway, we thought we'd surprise our dads by buying the garage. So we made Mr. Ryan an offer. It was not as much as he wanted. And probably not what it was worth. But he was desperate for cash, so he took it. Then we agreed to give him a percentage of what we made for the next ten years. Which we did. We wanted to give the shop to our dads. We were even planning to change the name to something like Ramon and César's, in their honor."

"Cool!"

"No, it was not cool. When we told our dads, they were furious. *Aye!* Hector and I almost cried. We were, how do you say … devastated. Here we thought they would treat us like heroes. And instead, they treated us like … like … like we had burned down that stinking garage instead of bought it. *'Let me tell you something,'* my father said to me, *'if you think this makes you better than me, it does not! I am the father, not you!'* I can hear his voice to this day, clear as a bell. I wish we could have backed out of the deal, but by then, it was too late. Mr. Ryan needed the money too badly. So we went through with the purchase. My relationship with my dad was never the same after that. Both he and my uncle quit soon after that. He even made us promise not to change the name from Ryan's Auto Repair. So we never did. He said that he would never want to disrespect him like that."

"*Dag*, Papi'," I said, looking at him with my mouth wide open. "I don't know what to say."

"There's nothing *to* say, Machito. The truth is, that my father could never be happy for me if he thought I would be more than him. But if I had worked in the shop, like he did his whole life, we would have been fine. But our relationship was never the same, up until the day he died."

Wow, what do you say to your dad after he just tells you why he and his dad stopped talking? Like what do you do with that? I had no clue, so

I said nothing.

"Machito, it's *muy importante** that you know you have my permission to be more than me. That's why you have to promise me that you'll stay in school. Promise me that you'll try harder. Remember where we came from. Remember how our family went from coming all the way from Puerto Rico, to getting a job in a repair shop, to *owning* that repair shop. Promise me you'll be more. Por favor, *m'ijo*."

"Well … okay, Papi'. I'll try." I said to him.

"Use you head, not just your hands. As your father, I will try to give you all that I can, but the one thing I will never ever give you, my son, is my permission to be *less* than me!"

71% OF STUDENTS REPORT INCIDENTS OF BULLYING AS A PROBLEM AT THEIR SCHOOL. — DoSomething.org

* Very important.

28

"RECESS" PIECES
— *by Mina Madsen*

For the first time ever, I don't feel like playing four-square today. Not sure if it's the whole Martian thing, or if I'm afraid that if I play, some giant monster will come and hit me with a fireball. But whatever it is, I'm not playing. And I'm the one who even played when I broke my arm last year. They all thought they could beat me 'cause I had my arm in a cast, but I showed them that was DEFINITELY NOT THE CASE. I creamed everyone that day.

So instead of playing, I looked for the others. I just had to talk to someone about this. The first one I saw was Bobby. He was alone at the tetherball court just punching the ball.

"Hey, Bobby."

"Hey, Mina."

One by one, the other three came over when they saw us. So there we were, the five of us standing in a circle staring at each other. Some kid named Carson came over to play tetherball, but we all stared at him until he got the message and left.

I don't remember who said what, but basically it was stuff like: What are we going to do? Did you tell anyone what happened? What do we do when we see Principal Marshand today? Should we tell the police? And most of all, would anyone ever believe us?

Then it was quiet again. A real uncomfortable quiet. It was driving me crazy. Finally I broke the silence.

"I had, *like*, the weirdest dream last night?"

Everyone's eyes opened as big as pancakes!

"Me, too!" they all yelled at almost the same time.

"What was yours about?"

So I told them the whole story. Running from a monster with a flaming four-square ball, then being six-inches tall and running from Joy's stupid cat. Plus the Martian uniform ... having black hair instead of blonde ... eating Lucky Charms ... Everything that I could possibly remember.

"It was so real! Then when I woke up, it was like it actually happened!" I said.

"Tell me about it!" said Kimmy. Then she told us all about *her* dream where people were writing bad stuff about her on a wall.

"You mean like on your Facebook wall?" asked Bobby.

"No, a real wall," she answered. "But now that I think of it, maybe that's why the colors looked so familiar, maybe that's what it represented. *Hmmmm*."

Then, just like my dream, she had a second part to it, but instead of being little like me, she was super thin. Not like a supermodel, but like a paper doll. And she had on her Martian uniform too, and her face was weird. Then she dreamt that she slipped through the window of her room and ended up in the park. Some other stuff happened, but it wasn't as dangerous as almost being eaten by a giant cat. But unlike my dream, when she woke up, there was no proof that any of it had ever happened.

Dex couldn't remember his at first. But the more he tried, it slowly started to come back to him. He dreamt that he read every book in his house. Then when he was done, he even went online to read some more. Boring! Besides, if Dex is reading, it MUST have been a dream! When he woke up, most of the books in his house were in his room.

"Did you look any different?" asked Kimmy. "Like, in my dream, my hair was different, and my lips were really full. Kind of like Buck's."

"Yeah, now that I think of it, my hair was really short, bro'," answered Dex. And I had that uniform on and those big goggle-things that I tried on."

"But wait, so far both me and Kimmy had dreams that were in parts. *Like*, the first part of mine was the monster, then the second part, when I was in the uniform, my hair was black and I was really tiny. Was yours in parts, too?" I asked.

"Uh … yeah, I think it was … Yeah! In the first part, I was in class, and I knew the answer to every question that they asked me. And the more I answered, the more the other kids in the class got mad at me. Then finally, they got so mad that they jumped on me and started beating me. Even Miss Brea got in a few punches. It was crazy!"

"Wow, that's hard to believe," said Kimmy.

"Yeah, Dex knew the answers. Wow!" said Buck with a big smile on his face. Then he told his story. Buck had a dream that all the kids in the cafeteria were insulting him and he couldn't think of anything funny to say back. But that didn't seem so odd if you ask me. Now, the second part was strange though. He had huge metal beaver teeth and three long red braids.

When he woke up, his pillow was shredded and it looked like his headboard had been attacked by a chainsaw! He thought his sisters had played a joke on him. His parents are still trying to figure out who to punish.

But I think the most damage came from Bobby. He also didn't really remember much, but when he woke up, the legs to his bed had snapped off and his mattress was flat against the floor. Plus all the food in his fridge was gone! Even something called *kimchi*, which none of us have ever heard of. His family didn't know *what* to think, so they grounded his brother Bryce.

"Did you have a first part, too?" I asked.

"Yeah, I think some big kids gave me a wedgie, but I don't really remember," he said.

We talked about our weird dreams and how much water we all drank last night. Finally the bell rang, that meant that recess was over.

"So, these *are* just dreams? Right?" I asked.

"I guess so ..." said Dex, "But who took all the books off my shelf? That was no dream."

"And what happened to my pillow and headboard? It seems like kind of a *co-inky-dink* that there is real evidence that it happened, don't you think?" asked Buck.

"Yeah, and who locked up my sister's cat and ate the Lucky Charms?" I added."

"And who ate all the food in my fridge?" asked Bobby.

"Could have been Kimmy!" answered Buck.

By the time she turned to hit him, he was halfway to class!

"You just wait, Buck Bievers! You just wait!" she yelled.

Then we all hurried to class. Mainly so we could get far enough away from Kimmy to laugh at Buck's joke. You know, sometimes he actually IS *kinda* funny!

29
STICKS AND STONES
— by Kimmy Kampbell

At 3:00 we all grabbed our stuff and headed back to detention. That's where we were supposed to go all week from 3-4 p.m. Fine by me, since I get to miss sports. But Bobby is not too happy about missing soccer practice all week. Oh well, guess that's why they call it detention and not recess. Principal Marshand was already there waiting for us.

"I'm assuming that you have a thousand questions for me, so let's have them," he said. So that's what we did. But first we told him everything that happened to us. You know, our weird dreams, what we were worried about... Everything. He looked pretty uncomfortable hearing about it.

"Did I really slip through the window of my miniva ... I mean ... my room?" Boy did I almost let the cat out of the bag! I can't believe I just did that! "If so, can I be that skinny ALL the time? Well not quite THAT skinny, but I'd love to be able to control it."

"It's as I feared, you have all begun to have physical transformations. That might be why your bodies required so much water. But that's just a guess at this point."

"You mean we're, *like*, Transformers now?"

"Yeah, we're more than meets the eye."

"Especially Kimmy!" said Buck.

"Whoa!" as soon as he said that my eyes started burning and I couldn't help blinking them like crazy. "What's happening?" I asked, starting to freak out a bit. "I feel dizzy. And my eyes are all blurry."

They all gathered around me and made me sit down. In a few minutes I was back to normal. Principal Marshand got me a glass of water just to make sure. Once I gave the thumbs up sign, he started talking again.

"As long as Miss Kampbell is feeling better now, I'll try to explain. As I mentioned before, on my planet, the orb bonds our body and our spirit and our mind. From the time of birth, we are taught to cherish them and take care of them individually and as a whole. In other words, just as I exercise my body and eat healthy food to nourish it, I also exercise my mind and put good things in it. Reading, learning, peaceful thoughts. A healthy mind and body help to create a healthy spirit ... Then when I use the orb, it acts as a healer. Like when you run a virus scan on your computer. It deletes bad stuff and gets everything else working at its best. So the healthier I keep my body, the more healthy it makes my mind and vice versa. Then once all three are working at their best, it allows them to fix themselves."

"Do you use it every day?" asked Bobby.

"No, but after a full day of running behind the five of you, and the stress that I felt from your actions as well as the empathy for your victims, I'm afraid that took a lot out of me."

"Was that in English or Martian?" asked Dex.

"Now as far as you are concerned, between your human DNA, and your toxic lifestyles, there's no way to even guess what it's done to you. You eat junk. You think junk. You treat each other like junk. You eat food that sickens your bodies. You do activities that rot your brains. So what the orb has done to you is anyone's guess. Mentally or physically."

"Physically? So wait, you ARE saying that those weren't dreams?! That REALLY happened to us last night? That stupid glowing thingy made us all into our worst fears or something? It turned us into the stuff we hate!" said Dex.

"Wait a minute, are you saying it made me fat *'cause* it thinks I hate fat kids?" asked Bobby.

"Well you *do* pick on Reggie," said Buck.

Just then the door opened and two boys walked in. I think one's name was George or Nate, the other was Oliver or Ian or something like that. Who knows? I don't like them anyway!

"*Ummm* … they told us we had to serve detention today," said one.

"Matt and Nick? Exactly what did you do?" asked the Principal.

Wow, I'm terrible with names, my guesses were really off!

"Nothing! We're innocent! It was Seve and Blake!"

"Then why are you here?" asked the Principal again.

"We don't know! It must be a mistake!"

"Okay, I believe you, you're both free to go!"

"Really?!" They both turned and ran out the room.

"Hey!" we all screamed at once, "How come you didn't believe us when we said *we* were innocent?"

"Because you're *not* innocent!" he said.

Oh, well I guess that's a good reason.

MY MISSION

— *by Principal Marshand*

"Well, I've already explained my Martian heritage. And I've told you about my mission. I assure you, it's completely peaceful. We were mainly scientists onboard, and a few *Orderons*, they are in charge of our security. But as I said, it was mainly scientists who were sent to Earth to study it in order to try to replenish our own ecosystem."

"How many were there?"

"A dozen scientists, and eight *Orderons*."

"So where are they now, do they all work here at the school? Is Miss Mary one of them?"

"No, there was a fight. It seems that one of our younger scientists named Gregor Re' didn't just want to study earth, he wanted to conquer it! While on our way here, he began to develop a virus that would attack humans, but leave your other earthly organisms unharmed. Then, instead of bringing back specimens to cultivate on our planet, we would all migrate here and become the new Earthlings. When we learned of his plan, we alerted the *Orderons* to arrest him. Unfortunately they were not able to do it before he set off explosive charges in our engine room. Our ship was blown apart, and was sent spiraling towards Earth. I am the only survivor."

"Wow, that's deep. So what happened to the ship?" asked Kimmy.

"You're standing on top of it!" I answered.

Dexter's eyes popped wide open. "Really? You mean your underground lab is part of your ship?"

"Yes. Our ship crashed with such force that it created a crater 200-feet deep."

"Wait a minute, why didn't anyone see the ship?"

"I used my lasers to move the surrounding dirt to cover it up. Years later, I decided to build this school on top. What better way to study humans and the Earth than at a school?"

"Wow, that must have been a long time ago. When did all that happen?"

"April 10, 1959," I answered again.

"Dude, you're old! How come you don't look it?"

"I can use the orb to gradually age my appearance. So when I calculate that I'm too old to function by Earth's standards, I simply use the orb to change my appearance completely. Then I just pretend that I am a new head of school. I even throw myself a retirement party and name a building after myself."

"So, you mean to tell me that you replace yourself? Hey, does that mean that you're also Principal Shinmar, my dad's old head of school?"

"That I am. As well as Principal Martin and Headmaster Morton."

"SHINMAR? That's Martian sideways, *kinda*. And Martin! And Morton. Now Marshand?!!! *'sta loca!* Not too subtle, are you?"

"Well who said Martians can't have a sense of humor? Must all aliens have big heads, long skinny arms and eat humans?"

"Hey wait a minute, wasn't Principal Martin an African American?"

"As a matter of fact, he was. Or I guess I should say, "*I was.*" I thought the school was ready for an African-American head of school."

"So what happened?"

"Well apparently they were *not* ready. I seemed to have overestimated the school's commitment to diversity. The board of directors made me resign after only one semester. Apparently I wasn't doing a good job," I said sadly.

"But I don't get it, it was still *you!* They were *all* you. You've been doing the same job for, *like*, 50 years. You started this school."

"Yes, Mina. I did. The only difference was the color of my skin. Quite literally. It was a very eye-opening experience."

"See? I *told* you that stuff happens. Now you guys know what I go through as one of the few black kids in this school," said Buck. "Do you know what it's like to talk about the Civil Right's Movement or slavery in class and have EVERYONE, including the teacher, turn and look at me? It's embarrassing! Just because I got accepted to attend this school, doesn't mean that I'll ever *really* be accepted here. There's a big difference. A *big* difference!"

"For me, too!" said Dex. "You might have to wait another 50 years before you can be a Latino head of school."

None of us, including me, knew what to say. We just looked down at our feet, or up at the ceiling. Anywhere but at Buck or Dexter. Finally, Mina broke the awkward silence. Thank goodness!

"So what's your real name, you know, like, your Martian name?" she asked.

"Gerolk Raf," he said. "My last name would be too difficult for you to pronounce. In fact, I'd have to remove your tongues in order for you to say it correctly."

"Really?!!!" they all said while covering their mouths. You should have seen the looks on the faces!

"Gotcha!" I said dryly.

"Oooh, can you let us shoot your laser gun sometime?"

"Sorry, Buck, but that ran out of power 20 years ago. Luckily I was able to adapt my ship's power source to use your electricity. Not enough to get it to fly, but enough for the lights and my computers."

"What's the fashion like on Mars? Do all of your clothes shrink to fit your body?" asked Kimmy.

"Speaking of which," I started, "Where are my uniforms?" There are five missing from my case.

"We don't know. We had them on, but they all, *like,* disappeared right off our backs. It was freaky!

I stared at them one by one to see if any of them would crack under the pressure. They didn't.

"So, *like,* what happened to the dude who blew up your ship?"

"Gregor Re´? I never saw him again. I assume he perished with the others."

"So how come you're still here? Why haven't you phoned home and had them come pick you up?"

"Our mission wasn't quite sanctioned by our government."

"Uh, was that in English or Martian?"

"He meant that he and his crew stole that ship and decided to do this mission on their own, Buck. Right, Principal Marshand?"

"Very good, Dex. Yes, something like that. So with my radio damaged, and the political battles that are probably still being fought on my planet… well let's just say that I no longer have any hope of ever being rescued."

"Can you change your face to look like anyone?"

"Not exactly. And it takes months to do so. And it's not exact. I can make my features larger or smaller but I couldn't make myself look like

Leonardo DiCaprio. It's more like how a caterpillar can transform into a butterfly as opposed to how the shape-shifters do it in the movies."

"Oh, you mean like Mystique from the X-Men movies?"

"C'mon, Buck, our principal doesn't know who the X-Men are!"

"Yes, it takes me almost the entire summer, that's why I always wait for school to end to resign or retire. Then by September, I'm ready to assume my new role. And by the way Cyclops, Wolverine, Storm, Beast, and Jean Grey who started as Marvel Girl then became Phoenix ... I most certainly, DO know who the X-Men are, Mr. Bonderman."

"Oh. So does the orb give you these weird powers, too? Like can you grow or shrink or whatever?"

"No, my changes are very slow and subtle. As I mentioned, it's more of a healing of body, spirit and mind. Obviously, it has affected your human bodies much more drastically. I'd like to test your blood before you leave today."

"Blood test?! Nobody told me there would be a test today. I didn't even study."

"Yes, Mr. Bievers. I get your joke. It's actually quite funny."

I decided to take them back to my lab in order to conduct the test. As soon as I had drawn blood from the last of them, the 4 o'clock bell rang, meaning it was time to send them home. And not a moment too soon. They bickered the entire time. And when they were not bickering, they were asking questions. Everything from, "What do we eat on Mars," to "Have I ever met John Carter?" The guy the movie was based on. I told them I had. They were impressed.

They even bickered about what questions to ask. Then they asked me questions *while* they were bickering. I couldn't wait for them to all go home. But for me, this is my home. I spent the next few hours studying their samples. There was definitely a change in each of them. A mutation in their DNA. Not a good sign, something as significant as this would be the difference in determining if their change was going to be temporary ... or permanent!

31
TAG, YOU'RE NOT IT!
— *by Kimmy Kampbell*

I don't even remember saying goodbye to everyone. Guess I was just kind of zoned out. I needed to do something to get my mind off of all this. When I opened my locker, the answer was staring me in the face. My pink sticky-note pad. Of course!!! Time for Kimmy's fashion tag tips. I grabbed the pad and a marker and headed down the hall. First person I saw was James. One glance was all I needed. I scribbled a quick note, walked over to him, and stuck it on his shirt. "You look awful in plaid," it said.

I kept moving. No need to stand around to talk about it. There's nothing to discuss. Next was Cameron. Write. Peel. Stick.

"Hey," he said. "What's wrong with my shoes?!"

"I don't have enough paper to explain it all. Let's start with the color. What's the matter, don't they make those for boys?" I said walking away.

Dahlia's note said, "braids don't work for you."

Sonali's said, "red is not your color."

Jacob and Grant got, "time for a haircut."

I was starting to feel better already!

Here are some of my others:

Robby: "stupid hat. No one thinks it's funny."

Scout: "How about trying colors that match?"

Gabriel: "Give your sister back her shirt."

Ben and Devin: "Read Jacob's note!"

And finally, for Rory I wrote, "Your jacket would look twice as good on me."

Ahhh, suddenly I felt much better. That always cheers me up! Before I knew it, it was time to go home.

Mom came to pick me up like she always does. But this time she parked towards the back like I asked her. It was the same place she dropped me off this morning. I had a lot longer walk, but I didn't mind. You know, I was actually glad to see her.

"Hey, Mommy, I'm not too hungry today, can we go shopping?"

"Well, hon …"

"Or can we go to our place? It's Thursday, right?"

"So it is. Sure, hon, we can go to our place, but let's go get our summer stuff out of storage first. And don't forget, the library closes at 5:30 today if you want to use their free Wi-Fi," said my mom smiling. She's pretty when she smiles, but that doesn't happen a lot.

So we started our afternoon. The storage place is never exciting, but I *did* get out some summer clothes and my good flip-flops. But the day got really good when we pulled up in the back of the church parking lot. The back door was open so we went downstairs. Recently we've been coming here once or twice a month, so the lady at the desk recognized us and smiled.

"I put something aside for you, young lady," she said while walking behind the counter. "I remembered you asked me about a few designers, and we actually got one in."

"Really?! Which one? Are they boots? Jeans? What? What?" I asked her impatiently.

"Here, you tell me!" she said handing me a bag.

"IT JEANS!!! *OMG!!!* I can't believe it. Please let them be my size, please, oh please, oh please!" I ran straight to the changing room. In a matter of seconds, I was out of my old pants and pulling up what would hopefully be my new jeans. Length is good. Now all I need to do is close them and ... YES!!!!! They fit!!!!!!!!!!"

I know that any of you boys who are reading this could probably care less, but, girls, you understand what a great find this was. Especially for *free!* I also got a cashmere sweater. It's a little warm to wear now, but it's a classic. I'll definitely be able to wear it in the fall. While I was there, they even let me plug in my laptop and cell phone to charge them up. I'll need my computer to do my homework today. It was such a great experience that I was sad to leave.

We headed back to the park afterwards to eat our sandwiches and a few apples that I took from the cafeteria. As always, I made sure that all of my homework was done before it got dark.

"Mom?"

"Yes, Kimmy?"

"Tell me about when you were a model again?"

"Oh, not that old story. Sweetie, that was *so* long ago. Even before I met your father."

151

"I know, but I like to hear it. Who did you work with again?"

"Well there was Elle Macpherson, Claudia Schiffer … oh and Jill Goodacre."

"Oh yeah. And who's she married to now?"

"Harry Connick, Jr."

"That's right. You have one of his CDs right?"

"I have a few of them, sweetheart."

"He seems nice. Whenever I see him on TV, he's always doing something nice for someone. That's the kind of man I hope to marry when I get older."

"But remember, Kimmy, I don't care how nice they seem …"

"I know, make sure I have my own bank account! I will. Okay, Mom, I'm listening, so start from the beginning of your modeling career."

"Yes, sweetheart."

And so she did …

32

FRIED BRYCE
— *by Bobby Bonderman*

Bobby

I got off the bus after sitting next to Buck again. I'm not sure if we're friends, but it's nice to have someone save me a seat for a change. We didn't talk about any Martian stuff *'cause* we didn't want anyone to think we were crazy. We mainly talked about stuff like video games. We like a lot of the same ones, so we finally set up a time to play X-box live.

The bus pulled up in front of my house like it always does. Sonic came out. My sister followed. We played soccer for a bit, then we went in. I had my fingers crossed that my mom didn't have another one of her celebrations prepared. Those are really hard to take. She came to the door to greet me, then her face turned sour as she saw Bryce's Lacrosse stick in the hallway.

"Oh, that boy! ..." she started.

But after the day that I just had, I really wasn't in the mood to hear them argue.

"Don't worry, Mom, I got it." I said before she could finish her sentence.

"Oooh, thank you, *Boobie*," she said running her hand against my cheek.

I plopped my backpack and soccer ball in their proper place, then headed upstairs with the Lacrosse stick. "Oh, I'd better write down Buck's gamer tag before I forget," I thought to myself. So I went straight to my room to find something to write with. After that I ate dinner, did my homework, then ran down to the family room to crank up the Xbox. Put on my headphones, signed on ... and bloop ... there it was, a friend request from Buck. Hey, maybe this means we *are* friends!

We played a bunch of stuff, some of it new, and some of it not so new like Halo 4 and Castle Crashers.

"Oooh, I'm *pwning* you, *noob!*" I said bragging.

"Hey, maybe we shouldn't play any games where we have to shoot aliens anymore," Buck's voice came through on my headset. "Those dudes might be Principal Marshand's cousins!"

We both cracked up. I don't know if it was because it was really all that funny, or because it was nervous laughter that we just needed to get out. But it was fun to laugh about our secret.

"You ever see someone laugh at a funeral?" Buck asked. "Man, my Aunt Jeannine and Aunt Donna do it all the time! One time they just busted out laughing, no one knew why. They couldn't stop, so they tried to *play it*

*Pronounced *po-ning*, remember? **154**

off like they were crying. Then one of the church ladies came over to try to soothe them. Started rubbing their backs. Made them laugh even harder *'til* they both had to get up and get some air. Everyone in the church thought they left because they were overcome with grief."

That's pretty funny. You know, Buck really is pretty funny when he's not trying so hard. Wonder if I do that, too?

Just then I heard a door slam followed by feet stomping. Sounded like they started on the top floor, went all the way down to the main floor, and are now coming down here. I hope Bryce isn't going to kick me off the Xbox. He swears it's his, but Dad bought it for all of us. But then again, he swears that Dad is his, too!

I looked over at the stairs just in time to see Bryce looking at me with fire in his eyes. What could I have done?

"What was this doing in *your* room?" he snarled while holding up his Lacrosse stick. "I was looking all over the house for this!"

"Oh, I can explain …" I started.

"Are you trying to steal from me, huh, are you?"

WHAP!

Ow! He slapped me in the head. My headphones fell to the floor.

"Hey! That hurt!"

"It was supposed to, *dweeb!* That's what happens to thieves in this house."

"But …"

But before I could say anything, he put me in a headlock and started yelling at me. "Oh, are *ya gonna* cry now, BOOBIE? Huh, is mama's *wittle* baby *gonna* cry his *wittle* eyes out?"

"Cut it out, Bryce!"

"Oh, tough guy, huh? Maybe you're *gonna* do a little karate on me? Huh, Bruce Lee? Are you *gonna* Karate chop me?"

"Bruce Lee was Chinese! I'm Korean!"

"Whatever! You just keep your hands *offa* my stuff … or else! Now say you're sorry."

"But …"

155

"Say, it shrimp. Say your sorry you stole from me!!!"

"Okay, okay, I'm sorry I stole your stupid stick!"

He loosened his grip and let me slump to the floor. I wiped the tears from my eyes. Then I heard Buck's voice coming from the headset.

"Bobby? Bobby? Are you okay? Who was that? Bobby?"

"Yeah, your girlfriend is just fine!" Bryce yelled so that Buck could hear him. "Just tell him to keep his greasy little mitts *offa* my stuff."

Then he stormed off. I waited until I heard the front door close before I started talking.

"Yeah, I'm fine," I said. "I just hate him so much!!!" We didn't talk anymore. We just played. I pretended all the aliens were Bryce. The Grunts, the Jackals, all of them!

After about half an hour, I heard his mom call him, so we said goodbye.

"I'll see you tomorrow, okay, Bobby?"

"Okay, Buck."

"And, Bobby?" he said.

Oh boy, here it comes, some long winded mushy speech.

"Yeah, Buck?"

"Try not to eat all the food in the fridge tonight. The rest of your family might starve to death!"

"Ha! Okay, Buck. Good night, dude."

"Later, man!"

You know, he really IS *kinda* funny!

33
PRESTO CHANGE-O
— *by Bobby Bonderman*

Bobby

When I got to school today, there were two things that I wanted to do. The first was to avoid Buck. Don't get me wrong, I like Buck now. I just didn't want to explain to him what happened last night. You know, that my brother likes to push me around. The other thing was that I really *kinda* wanted to see Reggie. Not sure why. It definitely wasn't to give him a wedgie, that's for sure. My wedgie-giving days just might be over. I asked one of the kids who hangs out with him, actually he's one of the *only* kids who hangs out with him, and he said Wedgie … I mean Reggie hasn't been to school in a few days. *Hmmm*, wonder if he's sick?

I did see Buck a couple of times here and there. No long conversations, just *kinda* like:

"Hey, man."

"Dude."

See, that's what I like about being a guy. We get to bury our feelings deep inside. Girls have to talk about everything. But us? We just keep it moving.

After a long day of school, I went to my locker to drop off my books before detention. So now you're almost caught up on the whole story. Principal Marshand came to my locker to get me. The others were already waiting for us in our usual dark, stinky classroom. We headed down to the hideout. There are quite a few entrances to the lab all over the school, so if there was someone in front of one of them, we just went to one of the others.

Kimmy started off, "I changed again last night, but I was able to change back when I wanted to. I actually think that I can do it whenever I want. *OMG!* It's awesome!"

"Really, you mean you can change back and forth at will?" I asked. "How did you do it?"

"I don't know, I guess I just concentrated. Guess that leaves you out, Buck! *Type type type and … send!*"

"Hey, nice flip-flops, Kimmy," said Mina. "I really like the gold color."

"Thanks, Mina. I like yours too. You always look good in red. Your nails, your feather … and I like your duct tape bracelet. Did you make it yourself?"

"Yep, I've made a bunch of stuff. I think my favorite is my wallet."

"I like you're little black ring, too. What kind of rock is that?"

"Uh, girls, can we get on with trying to see if we can control our powers? I mean not that playing 'the fashion channel' hasn't been the highlight of my day," said Buck.

So we tried it. 1-2-3-presto-chango. Nothing. We concentrated harder. 1-2-3-presto-chango ... Nope. Nothing. We all looked the same. Then we tried it again, 1-2-3-presto-chango. But this time Kimmy really did change! It was amazing!!! She was super thin and in that uniform!!! Dude, it was the weirdest thing I've ever seen in my entire life!!! She looked like an alien!!! Even more than usual!

"Whoa, you're flat as a pancake! Kimmy, that's freaky!"

"*'sta loca*!!!!!"

"Dag!"

"*Like*, that's *like ... like ...* unbelievable!"

We all just stared at her. She was the weirdest looking thing I have ever seen. EVER!!! Even weirder than Lady Gaga! Principal Marshand stared at her, too. Then we couldn't help but go over and touch her. She was paper thin, but she was solid. Like she got rolled over with one of those steamroller things that pave the streets. Dex tried to pick her up, but he couldn't, so I guess she weighs the same as she usually does.

"*'sta loca!*" he said. "That *is* freaky!"

"Oooh, nice hairdo, Kimmy. It's cool the way it covers your eye. And it's black! Your hair, not your eye. What happened to your red hair?"

"I *dunno*," she said. "Everytime I change, my hair looks like this."

"Well it looks really nice," added Mina.

"Wait a minute. She's a thin as a piece of paper and all you notice is her hair?! ... Girls are crazy!"

"But, I love how cool I look. The jet-black hair that covers one eye. And I have to say, I absolutely love my *lips!* They're so full, like I had them done, right?"

"Actually," I said, "if you ask me, they look like Buck's lips."

Everyone looked at Kimmy, then looked at Buck. And back again.

"Yeah, you're right, Bobby. She *does* have Buck's lips," said Mina.

"I guess you're right, I do. Thanks, Buck! And I'm especially thankful that I don't have your ears!"

"Hey, what's wrong with my ears?" asked Buck.

"And your nose is different too. *Kinda* like my nose, a bit," added Mina.

We looked at Kimmy, then we looked at Mina, then back again.

"You're right. So you've got Mina's nose and Buck's lips ... and hey, you have *my* jet-black hair," I said.

They looked at me, then at Kimmy, then back again.

"And you're wearing one of my missing *Orderan* uniforms! I was wondering when you'd confess to stealing them."

"But, *like*, we didn't steal them, they just *kinda* vanished!"

Well it may have been freaky, but once everyone saw how she looked, we all wanted to do it too! I know, weird, right? So we concentrated harder. 1-2-3-presto-chango. 1-2-3-presto-chango. 1-2-3-presto-chango. Buck was next!

"*Dag!* He's a werewolf!" yelled Dex.

He wasn't far off, either. If we thought Kimmy was freaky, Buck was just as bad, if not worse! His two front teeth grew to, like, four inches long and looked like they were made of steel. And he was in his costume too, even the mask. Oh, and we found out what happened to Kimmy's long red braid. They were on Buck's head! But he had three of them. And they were bright red, like stop signs.

"Dude, you've got red dreadlocks! And you're in the uniform."

"Red dreads! And look at those two big teeth, bro! You look like a mutant SpongeBob!"

"I call my new hairstyle *redlocks!*" said Buck. Although it's kind of hard to really understand him with those enormous teeth.

So now we tried to figure him out. Meanwhile Principal Marshand was just taking it all in, and saying nothing.

"Okay, he's got Kimmy's red braids, and Dexter's nose. And he's not brown anymore, he's like us," said Mina.

"You know what that means?" asked Kimmy.

"I can catch a cab when I go downtown?" joked Buck.

"No, the orb took all our features and scrambled them up."

"Maybe because we touched it at the same time!" I said.

"Interesting theory," added Marshand.

Now Mina and Dex tried even harder. 1-2-3-presto-chango. Mina was next, you know she would die if she was last. We heard a poof, then she was gone!

"*OMG*, she disappeared!" shouted Kimmy. She was right. I looked at where she was, and there was no one … until I looked down.

"Look!" I said pointing at the floor, "She shrank! … and she's black!"

There she was, in uniform like the other two, but she was only six inches tall, and African-American.

"Aw … she's so cute!" said Kimmy. "And look at her hair, it's puffy like two big mouse ears! And she's even shorter than Bobby!"

I shot her a look.

Now it was like a contest to see who could guess whose features she had.

"Dexter's curly hair … and … my nose … and …"

"Well obviously Buck's skin color and his ears!" interrupted Kimmy.

"Yes, those are definitely Buck's ears," said Dex.

"Hey, what's wrong with my ears?" asked Buck again.

Although it looked like Mina was talking, we couldn't really hear her. So Kimmy bent down to pick her up.

"I told you I was little," Mina said to her.

"You're like a little mouse, aren't you?" Kimmy replied.

1-2-3-presto-chango. Then it was Dex, his wasn't so freaky though. Besides his costume, he was in those big goggles again. And the funny thing was he had an afro! Like from the movies back in the 1970s! And acne.

"Wow," said Buck with a lisp, "you look like my dad's high school yearbook picture."

"Buck's hair, just a lot more of it, and his nose and Bobby's acne …" said Kimmy. "… and my mouth!"

"*C'mon*, Bobby, it's your turn."

"Yeah, come on, Bobby!" they all yelled, cheering me on. I was really nervous. What if I was the weirdest of all? At least some of them knew what they looked like, but I never saw what I looked like. I just know I ate a lot and was so fat that I broke my bed.

"Bob-by, Bob-by, Bob-by," they all chanted.

Oh, well, here it goes. 1-2-3-presto-chango. And finally it was my turn. But, to be honest, I didn't really want to change. But I did.

BLLURPPP!

"*Ugh!* What a disgusting sound," someone said.

One by one, their mouths dropped open, like baby birds waiting to be fed. No one said a word.

"Well?" I asked trying not to look down.

"You're, like … like 300 pounds!!!"

Really? That would be cool if I was as tall as the Hulk, but no such luck, I'm still kid-sized.

"WOW! You're, *like*, FAT!!! I mean *really fat!*"

We just stood there looking at each other.

I looked at my legs, they were huge. I lifted my arms, one by one. Blubber, as far as I could see. I looked at them looking at me.

Dex broke the silence, "Dude, you look like an anime Eric Cartman!" He busted out laughing before he even finished his sentence. And so did everyone else.

"Hey!" all of a sudden it felt like someone gave me a wedgie. I turned around, but no one was there. "Ooohhh, wedgie!" I yelled. Boy that really hurt. But if I had to take it, I was also going to dish it out. "Well look at your face, Dex, anyone want to play connect the dots?"

Now it was Dex's turn to flinch. "Brain freeze!" he yelled.

"What?"

"*Bro*, it felt like I just got a brain freeze. You know, when you drink something cold too fast?"

I turned around to see if there was something shiny enough where I could see my reflection. I ran over to the glass cases where we took the uniforms from. And when I saw what I looked like, it was like someone punched me in the stomach. Fat body, round face, big spikey blonde hair (I guess I got that from Mina), and Kimmy's turned up nose. Dex was right, I looked like I ate *Yu-Gi-Oh!* One by one they all ran over to get a glimpse of themselves.

For the next 10 minutes, we did nothing but stare at each other and talk, and all at the same time. So no one knew what anyone was saying. When he couldn't take our babbling any longer, Principal Marshand stepped forward.

"Enough," said Principal Marshand.

"Oh, *c'mon, bro*. Look at these thick goggles!" complained Dex. "They look like Coke bottles. But when I take them off, everything looks blurry. Aw, man. I'm stuck with these things. Are these really the best optical enhancements you could find? I'm *gonna* look like a *noob!*"

"Did you just say 'optical enhancements'? And don't worry, dude, look at us, we *all* look like *noobs!* Big buck teeth, obese, pimples, super skinny, six-inches tall …"

"Yeah, we look like the chess club!" said Buck with a lisp.

That might have been really funny if we weren't all freaking out.

"Hey, I really *do* have *buck* teeth! Literally! Get it? My name is Buck… And these are my teeth. Buck teeth?"

"Yeah, and now you're finally funny, Buck," said Kimmy.

"Really?"

"Funny looking!" she said.

"Ow, toothache!" he said flinching. "How did that happen? Why do we keep getting these weird pains? And what about you, Kimmy? You went from fat-girl to flat-girl!"

Kimmy sat down holding her head. "*OMG*, what's wrong with me?"

"Where do we start?" asked Buck.

"Kimmy, are you okay?" asked a concerned Principal Marshand.

"I *dunno*," she said, "it's like everytime Buck talks, I get a headache."

"Who doesn't?" shot Dex.

"Ow!" said Buck as he put his hand up to cover his teeth.

"What's wrong?"

"I got a toothache again! *Ooohhh* ... I mean it only lasted for a second, but man, it sure hurt while it did," he said.

"Whoa, hold up, let me try something, *bro*," interrupted Dex. "Okay... ready? ... Buck, you're the funniest guy I know."

"Thanks, Dex."

"Funny *lookin'*, that is!"

"Ow!" he shouted while putting his hand up to his teeth again.

Next, Dex looked at Kimmy. "Kimmy, I think you have a really cool fashion sense."

"Duh! Well that's not really a news flash, Dexter, everyone knows that," she said.

"Which is good because you don't have any common sense!"

As soon as he said that, Kimmy closed her eyes and got real quiet.

"*Like*, are you okay, Kimmy?"

"I *dunno*, I just feel dizzy again all of a sudden."

"Hey, Mina," said Dex looking in her direction. "I won't say you're boring, but when you're on the playground, they should change the name of the game to FIVE-squares!"

Just like me, Kimmy and Buck, something happened to Mina. Not anything too painful, but enough to make her grab her neck like she had a sore throat. Weird, huh?

"What's going on?" we all wanted to know.

We looked at the principal, but he said nothing. Finally Dex started talking. "Okay, well even though I can't explain it, it looks like our hurtful words really are *hurtful* ... you know, literally!"

Dex might be on to something.

"Let me try," said Kimmy. "Oh, Principal Marshand," she sang ... "What do you have in common with my fashion sense? ... Give up? They're both out of this world!"

"That's not insulting," said Buck. "And it's not even funny!"

"What? Well I'll show *you* insulting! Listen to *this:* I can't imagine anyone doing a worse job as principal. You pick on kids just because they're popular, your suits are probably out of style on *two* planets and most of all, you're *boring*! There, that *oughta* do it!" We all stepped back to look at him. But nothing happened. I mean nothing.

"Thank you for sharing, Miss Kampbell," he said.

"No problem."

"And by the way, that little outburst just earned you an extra day of detention."

"What?! But it was a test, you know, an experiment!" she protested.

"Regardless, I'm still your principal, and you must learn to respect me. You human children can be so rude sometimes."

"Okay, so wait a minute," interrupted Mina who had to almost scream for us to hear her. "So then it's not that our painful words hurt others, it seems like painful words only hurt US!"

"You mean sticks and stones may break our bones PLUS words will hurt us, too?" asked Buck.

"So, *like*, we can't insult each other? What fun is that?"

"I think it's more than that," said Principal Marshand. "It looks to me like the orb has tapped your subconscious and transformed you into the people that you disrespect the most."

"So ... *like* ... I hate short people?" asked Mina in her little tiny voice. "That's not true."

"No, not physically little, but I believe the term I heard you use a few days ago was MOUSEY. Kids who don't speak up for themselves. Kids who simply blend into the background," added Principal M.

"Well, I guess I do ... now that you mention it," said Mina. "I call kids mousey, so now I shrink as small as a mouse. And I'm quiet as a mouse. That stinks!"

"But you're SOOO cute!" said Kimmy.

"Well I definitely hate those *stringbing* showoffs," she added. "They think they're so cute because they're as big as my finger. But now ... I am, too. *Sigh!*"

"Maybe it thought you hated pancakes, that's why it made you flat," said Mina.

"Oh, please, does Kimmy *look* like she hates pancakes?" said Buck.

She got another dizzy spell.

"*OMG*, I'm really going to have to get used to this. Either that or I'm going to have to kill Buck by the end of the day," she said.

"So wait," starts Dex. "Since I was up all night reading, is it saying that I'm afraid to be smart, or that I hate smart kids?"

"Probably both," said the Martian.

Then it was Buck's turn to figure out what happened to him. "Well, I DO hate bad teeth! But can you blame me? Both of my parents are dentists! I hear them talk about bad teeth all day. Like they say 'the tooth hurts?' Get it? Instead of 'the truth hurts'?"

"And I pick on fat kids," I added looking at the floor. "*Sigh* ... Now I'm fatter than all of them."

"Furthermore," Principal M added ...

"Ohhhh, you mean there's more? Isn't looking like a circus side show enough?"

"Well, as we all see, somehow it also looks as if it scrambled your DNA a bit. So you basically swapped features."

"Yo, Bobby, your hair is cool. You look like a cross between Goku and Pikachu, or one of those anime characters, dude," said Buck.

"Well good, that will make it harder for people to recognize us if anyone ever sees us in public."

"Recognize us?! *Shoot*, do you think I'm ever going to let *anyone* see me in public looking like this? Even if my hair *is* cool, the rest of me is fat!" I said.

"Yes, it must be hard for a kid your age to come to school everyday, knowing that there are people waiting to tease you. It probably doesn't do much good for one's self esteem. Does it Bobby?" asked Principal M. looking at me. We both knew he was talking about Reggie. *Sighhhh* ... Now I feel even worse.

"Hey, Kimmy, I guess you really are a *stringbing* now. Isn't that what you call everyone?" Dex said.

"Oh, so now we're coming up with names for everyone, huh? I guess since you read a few books for once you think you're a real *knowitall*."

"Well, so far we've got two names, *Stringbing* and *Knowitall*. Not exactly the Avengers, you know?" added Buck.

"Oooh, I got one for Mina. How about Mini something?" added Kimmy.

"I was thinking more like MEAN something …" Dex added.

"Nah, too close to her real name. I like Mini better."

Mina went to yell, like she usually does, but nothing came out. Just a whisper. It was the wildest thing. She cleared her throat and tried again. And again, the only thing that came out was a whisper. The louder she tried to talk, the softer her voice got. It's a miracle!

"Hey, how 'bout *Mini Mouth?*" Buck asked. "It's *kinda* funny 'cause it sounds like *Mini Mouse* but it's also the opposite of what she normally is, a *big mouth!* ZING! Right after he said that, Mina flinched. Oops, hurtful words, he forgot. But before he could apologize, everyone turned to him. "What? Plus her hair looks like mouse ears."

"Okay, Mr.-I-wish-I was-one-of-the-X-Men with big steel teeth. What do we call *you*?!"

"Well I got teeth like Wolverine's claws, but I looks more like a beaver!" he said. "How about *Beaverine?* After all, that's what I called Grace. So I guess it's only fitting."

"Hey no fair," said Kimmy, "you can't come up with your own insulting nickname! That's *our* job. I vote for Stupid Head!"

"Well, I kinda like Beaverine!" said Mr Loco (You know I mean Dex, right?)

"What are you guys *gonna* call me, Big Boy?!" I yelled. Hey if Buck can come up with his own nickname, maybe they'll let me choose my own, too.

"Oh, he's more than just big, look at him!" whispered Mina.

"Beefy Boy!"

Then Kimmy got in on the fun, "how about *Blubber Boy?!*"

"That's it!" said Dex, "you're *way* past big, *bro.* You got *mad* blubber."

"So what now, I mean we look like superheroes, so are we *gonna* fight crime? I don't think so. These names don't leave this room, right? I mean, it's cool to pretend and all, but it's not like I'm going to make us a sign that says, 'Here we are, the greatest superhero team in the history of the world:

Blubber Boy, Mini Mouth, Stringbing, Knowitall and the awesome *Beaverine!!!*" said Buck. "No way. This will be our little secret. Agreed?"

"Agreed!" said everyone.

"But while we're at it, can we come up with a name for our group. I mean, how cool would it be if we were the world's first real superheroes? I mean, not that we have any real super powers or anything, but as long as we're pretending, What harm would it do? ..."

"How about the Defenders?" suggested Buck. "That's kind of a cool name."

"Defenders?!!!" said Principal Marshand in a tone that let us know that he was about to give us yet another lecture. "You kids don't DE-fend anyone. If anything you're OF-fenders. You're the most offensive group of young kids that I've ever come across in all my years at this school. This may be your opportunity to use these gifts to make up for some of the awful ways that you've treated other kids, or your siblings, or even your parents."

Man, he sure knows how to kill a good time.

"Gifts?!!! Well I don't plan to use my *gifts* for anything except for maybe slicing apples or something. Other than that, I don't expect to be changing into this form after today." I think Buck spoke for all of us.

But for the rest of detention we just practiced seeing what we could do. You already know that Buck has long sharp teeth. But we wanted to see just how sharp. First they handed him a stick. *CHOMP!* Snapped it right in two. Then something bigger like one of those 2 x 4s. You know, the big pieces of wood? *CHOMP!*

They kept giving him things that were bigger and harder. He chomped them without even really biting down that hard. The last thing they gave him was a piece of metal. I'm not sure if it was iron or steel or what. But it was bigger than his leg. He had to bite down a lot harder this time. But then it started to bend ... and finally ... *CHOMP!!!* He split it in two.

"Awesome, this *Beaverine* thing might be pretty cool after all!" he finally admitted. "Maybe it *is* a super power."

Next up was Kimmy. She was so skinny, that when she turned sideways, we could barely see her at all! Wow, when they use their powers, we can't SEE Kimmy or HEAR Mina, there *is* a bright side!

Even though Kimmy was paper thin, she still weighs as much as she does when she's normal. And she was *kinda* strong too. I mean, not like the Hulk or anyone, but maybe like a grown man. She couldn't stretch or do anything like Mr. Fantastic from the Fantastic Four, but she could wrap around stuff like a … well … like the bandages the doctor wraps around your ankle when you sprain it. Pretty cool. And MUCH cooler than my stupid powers!

Mina was next. She was already about the size of a Barbie doll, but when she tried harder, *POOF*, she got even smaller. I mean really small, like the size of a mouse. Now *that* was freaky. Also *much* cooler than my stupid powers.

Dex spent the next 10 minutes showing off his brain. Man, was he smart all of a sudden. Still boring, but smart, so I'll spare you. But he still couldn't see when he took off the goggles. "Man, these stupid things must do *somethin'*, right?"

"Why don't you use that big brain of yours to concentrate real hard, maybe you can get it to do something," I said.

So he did. Focus … focus … focus … then *ZZZZZAAAAPPPP!!!*

A beam of light came shooting out of his eyes, bounced off one of the glass cases that our uniforms were in, then came back in our direction.

"Hit the floor!" someone yelled. So you'd better believe we did! Actually, it flew by so fast that by the time we ducked it was already past us. Finally it hit a bookcase and sent a few books flying.

"Cool! I have an Opti-Beam!" yelled Dex.

"A what?"

"Opti … it's a prefix. It means having to do with your eyes. So since the beam came out of my eyes, what else would you name it?"

"How about Barney?" Buck said. "Okay, now you *gotta* admit, THAT'S funny! Nothing. *Sigh* … I just thought it would be funny to name it Barney, that's all. Like if we were in the middle of a battle we could yell out, 'Dex, use Barney!' *Ugh*, it really wasn't worth the time it took to explain it."

I'd have to say, of all of our powers, my least favorite was mine. *Blubber Boy*. Wow, am I FAT!!!! And when I concentrated, I got even heavier. Not bigger, but heavier. I kept increasing my weight until the floor started to creak like I was about to fall through it. So I stopped.

Weird, right? And I had a weird smell, too. Not nasty, but … Buck

Bobby

said it was "like wet potato chips or something."

We played around with these "powers" until it was time to go. Principal M. warned us to be discreet. Meaning don't go showing them off. Well I can't speak for anyone else, but I know *I* sure won't!

Kimmy

Stringbing

Buck

Beaverine

Presto Change-O

Bobby

Blubber Boy

Mina

Mini Mouth

Dex

Knowitall

171

34

THE HURT LOCKER
— *by Kimmy Kampbell*

The next few days were pretty quiet. None of us had any more scary surprises in the middle of the night. But we still met at detention each day to practice changing and see what else we could do. We showed up at detention the following week too. All except for Bobby who missed a few days to go to soccer practice. But to be honest, I think he doesn't want to do it because he's, you know, fat. He's not handling that well.

But one day when I was on my way to detention, who do I bump into but Samantha and Tessa? My sworn enemies. They're the ones who got me into this whole mess in the first place, remember? If they didn't get me sent to detention that day, I would have never touched that stupid orb!

"Looks like it's time for detention again, huh, Kimmy?" said Stringbing Samantha.

"Yeah, Kimmy, what's it been, like two weeks? Guess you must be a regular by now."

"Hey, girls," I said, "all I know is that after I leave detention, I'll be going home to my nice big house, and playing with all of my great stuff. I have the newest iPad at home. And it's so new, I haven't even had a chance to take it out of the box yet. Oh, and I just got another pair of IT Jeans last week. Maybe I'll wear them for you tomorrow so you can see what they look like up close."

"Well I still think you're full of bologna," said Tessa.

"Yeah, well I'll bet my boots cost more than your whole wardrobe!" I shot back.

Then she wrote something down on a piece of paper and showed it to Samantha. They both laughed. It made me flinch a little. Tessa put the paper in her locker, then they both got their stuff together and went to catch the 3 o'clock bus. They were the last to leave the hallway, which meant that I was there all by myself. I looked around, yep, I was alone all right. And it was killing me that I didn't know what was on that piece of paper. I wish I could pick the lock so I could see it.

Wait a minute, maybe I don't have to even worry about the lock. I looked around one more time just to make sure that no one was around. Then I concentrated and *POOF!* I was thin. Now it was just a matter of slipping in between her locker door and the frame.

I start with my hand. Still a little too big, so I concentrated even more to make myself thinner. And it worked. I started again. Yep, so far so good.

Up to the elbow. Now my shoulder. Okay, the scary part is putting my head in. Almost … a little more. Once that was in, the rest was easy. Now to find the paper. I guess technically I shouldn't use my powers to do stuff like …

POOF!

Wait, what happened? I grew back to my normal size. *OMG!* I'm stuck! What am I going to do?

"HELP!" I yelled at the top of my lungs while kicking the door.

Will I have to spend the night in here? Will they ever find me? What if I *hafta* go to the bathroom? I tried to get thin again, but I couldn't!

It seemed like I was trapped for hours. Days even. Finally the door opened and it was Principal Marshand. Boy was I ever glad to see him!

"You missed detention today, Miss Kampbell."

"Yeah, I got stuck in here. So you could say that I actually did have detention."

"More like solitary confinement," said Buck.

"What happened?" he asked.

"I have to admit, I used my powers. But for some reason, it stopped halfway through."

"Maybe that's when your conscious kicked in, Miss Kampbell," said the Principal.

Suddenly there was a crackle sound followed by a flash of light. And that brings us up almost to the present.

 90 PERCENT OF 4TH THROUGH 8TH GRADERS REPORT BEING VICTIMS OF BULLYING.
— DoSomething.org

35

ALMOST BACK TO THE PRESENT (For real)
— by Buck Bievers

Buck

I looked out into the circle in front of our school and saw a bunch of kids running away from the cafeteria. Luckily it was a little after 4 o'clock so most kids were already gone. The main ones left were the ones coming from soccer and field hockey practice and who don't take the bus.

Then one lone figure came out of the door to the lunchroom. It was none other than Miss Mary, our head cook. Her skin was *kinda* green and she was floating off the ground about a foot or two in the air. Let me say that again: Her skin was *kinda* green and she was *floating* off the ground about a foot or two in the air! You have to admit, that's weird, right?!

"Somehow Miss Mary must have gotten ahold of the orb and it transformed her too," said our Martian principal. "But unlike you, it seems as if it has made her very aggressive. Stay here, I'm going to see if I can calm her down."

He disappeared out the door and headed to the circle to talk to her.

We pressed our faces against the windows to see what was happening.

"Miss Mary," he said, "What can I do for you?"

"Principal Marshand, I don't have *a beef* with you, but I have to teach these kids a lesson."

"Well, I can't let you do that, Miss Mary."

"Then I'm sorry, sir, *'cause* you've always been good to me. Most of the times, you're the only one. But these kids … *ooohhh* someone's *gotta* set them straight. And if you won't do it, then I *hafta* be the one."

And as Marshand opened his mouth, Miss Mary lifted up her arm and I swear it looked like spaghetti just shot out from her fingers! It wrapped him up like a mummy in just a few seconds! We all screamed. Well not me, the girls screamed.

"*Whoa!* She's got powers too!" said Mina.

"So what do we do?"

"We have to help him, don't we?"

There was a long silence. A REALLY long silence.

"Yeah, we do!" said Dex. "Let's change into our uniforms and see if we can stop her."

"But what if people recognize us?"

"How could they? We look completely different? Plus we even have masks on. But just remember not to call each other by our real names while we're out there."

"So what do we call each other, 'hey you'?"

"No time to come up with anything now, let's just use the funny names we came up with before."

"You mean *Stringbing* and *Beaverine* and those other names?"

"Look, it's the only thing we'll remember on such short notice, *bro.* Now *vamanos**!"

Dex concentrated until ... *POOF!* He turned into *Knowitall.*

Followed by: *ZING! WHOOSH! and FFFFT!*

Hey, what happened to *BLLURPPP*? Everyone changed, but Bobby.

"*C'mon*, man. Get fat already."

"Nah, you guys go on," he said.

"But, Bobby, you're one of us, you *have* to change," said Kimmy. "We need you."

"I ... I can't go out there like that. Everyone will laugh at me."

"Bobby, we don't know what we're up against. The old lady just shot spaghetti from her fingers, man! We're *gonna* need all the help we can get. *C'mon* ... what do you say ... *Blubber Boy*? Hey, if you do good, I'll put it on the Internet. Know where?"

"*YouTube?*" he asked.

"No, *YouTUB!*" I added. *Oops*, I forget, our words hurt. "Oh man, did I just give you that wedgie feeling?" I asked. "Sorry."

"Actually you didn't. Maybe it's 'cause I knew you were joking. Or because I consider you a friend now. Who knows? Okay, here it goes ..."

Then all of a sudden, *BLLURPPP!*

That sound was him changing. At least, I *hope* that's what that sound was. I put my hand out. Then *Knowitall* put his hand on top of mine. Then *Stringbing's* flat hand appeared, which, to be honest, still *kinda* freaks me out a little. I mean, she's like a cardboard cutout. *Eeeyewww!*

"Um ... guys. Down here," said a squeaky little voice from the floor. That was *Mini*. Obviously, she can't reach that high, so we all bent down.

* "You like looking down here, don't you?" **177**

Finally Bobby, I mean, *Blubber Boy* reached over with his fat little sausage fingers* and put his hand on top of the pile.

"Ready?" he asked.

"Ready as we'll ever be," I answered.

So we headed towards Miss Mary to see if we could stop her. And with all the weird things that have happened to us recently, fighting to save our school has *got* to be the weirdest!

* "Ha ha, made you look again!"   **178**

36

"MISS MARY, OUR HEAD COOK, IS NOW A SUPER-POWERED-VILLAIN INTENT ON DESTROYING OUR SCHOOL; AND THIS ISN'T EVEN THE STRANGEST THING THAT'S HAPPENED TO ME THIS WEEK"

— by Blubber Boy

Knowitall grabbed his skateboard and we ran out the door to help our principal and save our school. Well, three of us ran, *Knowitall* road his skateboard, and *I* just walked as fast as I could. Which was slow.

Then *Wham!* I looked over and *Knowitall* was laying flat on his back. He rubbed his head, then stood back up and got on his board again.

Wham! He fell off his board again.

"*'sta loca!*" he yelled, slapping the ground with his fist. "*Ow!* What's going on? I never fall off my board!"

He tried it one more time. This time he made it about five feet before, you guessed it — *Wham!*

"I guess now that you're so smart, you don't have your skateboarding skills anymore," I said.

He sighed, then struggled to pick up his board again.

"Man, and it's heavy too. It feels like it weighs a hundred pounds! What's going on?"

Then Buck, I mean *Beaverine*, walked over and picked it up without a problem. "Dude, you may be super smart now, but you're also super weak!"

"So what do we do now?!" I ask as the sweat drips from my forehead.

"Well how do I know?!" answers *Knowitall*.

"You're *supposed* to know, you're the smart one! That's why your name is *Knowitall*, remember?" says *Stringbing*. "Duh!"

"But we don't even know if she's bad yet." he answers back.

"Dude, look at her! You're telling me you don't notice the color of her skin?!" yells *Beaverine*.

"*OMG*, that's so racist! You can't judge someone just by the color of their skin! Don't you pay attention in life skills class? *You* of all people should know that, Buck! You're, you know, black," says *Stringbing*.

"Kimmy, Miss Mary *IS GREEN!!!!*" answers Beaverine. "I don't think whoever said 'not to judge people by the color of their skin' was talking about *green* people! Plus she's floating off the ground!!! *C'mon*, man, *gimme* a break! I think we can go out on a limb here and say she's *evil!!!*"

"But it's the lady from our cafeteria. It's not like she's green all the time. Maybe she just …"

"Ate some of her Sloppy Joes? Yeah right. And what about the floating part? A bad case of gas?" asks *Beaverine*.

So this is my new life. Fighting flying green people. I can't believe that I used to complain about how it was before. Compared to this, my brother Bryce, and even celebrating Korean day, is like a trip to Frankie's Fun Park! I'd give anything for it to change back. Back when they used to only call me Bobby. Now they call me *Blubber Boy! Ugh!* … I thought heroes were supposed to be cool!

I look over at Dex, I'll bet even he's scared now, and he's one tough kid. Then I look over at Principal Marshand who's all wrapped up and wiggling like a giant caterpillar. Man, he got totally *pwned* by an old lady.

I look at *Knowitall*, but he's new at this too, so he just shrugs his shoulders. Well that was a waste! Then we both look at *Stringbing*, she *always* knows what to do, or at least she pretends to always know what to do. Same reaction from her. We still can't see *Mini-Mouth* 'cause she's hiding in the grass somewhere, so we all look at *Beaverine*. He opens his mouth to say something. But before he does, we realize that he's probably about to say some sort of stupid joke, so we turn away.

"Forget you guys!" he says.

I don't feel like laughing right now. Instead I press both my hands against this new fat belly of mine to keep them from shaking. I rub along the river of pain that goes from my belly button all the way up to right below my neck. I try to swallow. But my throat is like a desert. Beads of sweat still drip down my forehead, past my eyes, and around my chubby cheeks like I just got out the shower. Luckily I'm not the only *noob* out here trying to save William Shatner Middle School from being destroyed by Miss Mary.

"Okay, guys, spread out!" says *Knowitall*, who I guess just figured out he has to be our leader now. We listen 'cause we don't know any better.

"*KK*," says *Stringbing*.

We do what he says. I lift one of my *ginormous* legs forward. It feels like it takes forever! Then I move the other one. There's a squeak sound as my thighs rub up against each other. Man, I don't know how kids like *Weggie* can do this. It's like moving in slow motion.

Suddenly Miss Mary points her fingers at us.

37

NOW YOU'RE ALL CAUGHT UP!
— *by Blubber Boy*

Miss Mary looks at me, I back up slowly and get ready to run. Then I realize that I probably can't run 'cause I'd probably look worse than when *Weggie* tries to run when we play dodgeball during gym He runs like some *sorta* chubby penguin. All the kids laugh. I don't think my tiny little legs will carry my fat body but so fast, so instead of running, I stand up straight and try to look mean.

"I told the school to stop serving you all so much junk. Pizza, french fries, soda pop … now look *atcha*," she said while shaking her head at me.

"But, it's not my fault," I said. Now just why I felt I needed to get the approval of a woman who is attacking our school, I don't know. But boy, this new body of mine has me really paranoid. It's awful.

"No, it's not your fault, you're just a kid. A fat one … but you're still a kid. It's the adults' fault, we're the ones who should be watching over you," she said.

Then she turned away. Who knows, maybe she felt sorry for me, because she decided to shoot at *Stringbing* instead. Cool!

"Turn sideways!" yells *Knowitall.*

"*KK!*" she says. Luckily she listens and does what he says. The spaghetti sails right past her.

Miss Mary raises her hands up again. I know it's *gonna* be my turn this time, 'cause she knows with me, she can't miss! The others are all fast. And *Mini Mouth* is still hiding in the grass since she's so tiny. Miss Mary probably doesn't even know she's around. Yep, she shoots at me, all right. Dude, I don't even try to run. What's the point? And I'd rather be wrapped up like our principal than have the kids who are watching us make fun of the way I run. I mean, they're already cracking jokes about each of us and we're here trying to save them! How's that for gratitude? *Oooh*, I sound like my mom. Sorry.

"*Blubber Boy*, watch out!" yells *Knowitall.*

I close my eyes and wait to feel that stuff wrap me up.

"*Knowitall*, use *Barney!*" yells Buck. I mean *Beaverine.*

Then I hear a sound like a giant bug zapper or something. You know, ZZZZZTTTT! Then a plop. I open my eyes and see a pile of sizzling spaghetti at my feet. Actually, it smells *kinda* good. I look over at *Knowitall* and see a little bit of smoke coming from his huge Coke-bottle glasses. Thank goodness for Barney!

"I prefer Opti-Beam, *not* Barney, thank you very much," he says as he points to his goggles. "Opt is a prefix that means 'pertaining to the eye.'" he says proudly. *Ugh*, he does that *all* the time. *So annoying.* But I give him a thumbs up anyway for saving me. Then I turn and give one to *Beaverine* for reminding him to use *Barney* in the first place.

"Like optic, or optical, or optometrist," *Knowitall* adds.

"What about the word option, huh, smart guy?" That's *Beaverine* doing what *he* does all the time.

"Can you shoot *him* next?" asks Kimmy, *oops*, I mean *Stringbing*.

"Gladly!" says *Knowitall*. "Come on *Blubber Boy*, let's surround her."

"Hey, did you just call him *Blubber Boy*?" asks one of the jerks hiding behind one of the cars parked in front of the main building. The rest of his knuckle-headed friends start to laugh. "He's so fat he can probably surround her all by himself!" They're *not* my friends so I start to get that wedgie feeling again. But I can't let on that I literally can't take a joke or they'll never stop.

I wait 'til no one is looking, then I slowly reach down and grab a wad of the fried spaghetti and put it in my mouth. I can't help it. When I'm big like this I have to constantly eat. And I can eat just about anything. Plus, the kids laughing at me made me nervous.

"*Eeeyewww!*" I hear coming from the same kid. "The fat kid just ate that weird stuff off the ground!" Then I hear a bunch more "*Eeeyewwws.*" I wish I could crawl into a hole. But first I'd have to find one big enough for me to fit in. I get that wedgie feeling again. So I guess it's not just insults that hurt, it's being embarrassed by people too. Just my luck.

We all take a step towards her, still not really knowing what to do. All we know is we have to do something 'cause she already trashed the kitchen and the cafeteria. The worst part is that we don't really know what to do. See, Miss Mary's really old so we don't want to hurt her. She might even be 100 or something! But I'm not that good at guessing how old adults are. My mom's still mad at me 'cause one day I told my teacher that my mom was 52 when she's only, like, 39 or something. Who knows! But since she's green and *floatin'* off the ground (Miss Mary, not my mom), maybe she doesn't know what she's doing. Like when Bruce Banner turns into the Hulk. So maybe she won't do anything bad. Maybe she'll just take a nap or something. Old people love to take naps.

Finally Miss Mary says something. "I been waiting for this day for a long time," she says, "now I'm *gonna* teach you *all* a lesson. A lesson that if you don't learn, it's *gonna* hurt ya! Hurt ya real bad!"

Gulp! ... Okay, at least now we know what she wants. She wants to teach us a lesson! Now what? Do I jump on her and use my enormous weight to flatten her like a pancake? *Mmmmm* pancakes ... Maybe *Knowitall* should shoot her with his Opti-Beam? And if he does, do we have to listen to him give us the meaning of the prefix "Opti" again?

Or *Stringbing* should just wrap her body around Miss Mary like a mummy and keep her that way *'til* the police come. That's if anyone actually called the police.

Lucky for us, it's also Miss Mary's first day as a super villain. As our school's head cook, she's always been a villain if you ask me, she just never had any superpowers until now. Unless you call making the entire school constipated a power. If that was the case, she'd be considered one of the most powerful beings in the entire universe! The "Galactus* of Gas!"

Suddenly she reaches into the pocket of her dingy gravy-stained apron and pulls out what looks like a ... a ...

"Is that meatloaf?" yells Beaverine. "Holy moly, she really DOES want to destroy the school!"

"Actually, her meatloaf isn't too bad. You should try it, it's kinda spicy!" says *Knowitall*.

She breaks it into five small pieces, drops them on the ground, then starts to mumble something in a language that doesn't sound like anything I've ever heard. All kinds of clicks and grunts and weird sounds.

"What the heck is that?" asks *Mini*.

"I think it's French!" answers *Beaverine*.

"That's not French!" snapped *Stringbing*, "And I know because I speak French."

Ugh, she's such a show-off! Anyway, before *Beaverine* can respond to her, the ground starts to shake. Like an earthquake!

"Stop jumping up and down, *Blubber Boy!*" says the *Beav*.

"Very funny!" I answer back. For some reason, his jokes don't give me that wedgie pain. "You're really funny, Beav."

"You think so?" he asks back smiling.

"Yeah, but *looks* aren't everything!" I say. *"Annnddd send!"*

"Hey, that's my line!" says an angry Kimmy, or whatever her name is again. *Stringbing*, I think.

The ground continues to shake. Next thing you know, these huge tree roots shoot up from the ground. Wait … not roots … they're … ARMS?!!! Whoa!!!

First one arm, then another. Coming up through the grass like zombies climbing out of a grave in one of those movies that still make me crawl into the bed with my mom even though I'm 11. (Man, I shouldn't have told you that.) And one-by-one, they all crawl out of the dirt and get in front of Miss Mary, who is still floating off the ground. But the zombies aren't regular zombie-types. You know, the kinds that walk real slow and eat brains like in the C.O.D. games. They don't look like people or zombies at all. They look like … like …

"My meatloaf minions!" says Miss Mary, adding a little evil cackle at the end.

"Sorry, Miss Mary, but we don't want to eat your meatloaf, and we definitely don't want your meatloaf to eat *us!* Hey, maybe you should call it Eat-loaf!" That's *Beaverine* talking.

"My minions will make you all listen to me!" Miss Mary yells while pointing at us!

All at once, the gravy-soaked creatures spread out to attack us. Dude, these meatloaf things are gross. I thought minions were supposed to be cute, like in Despicable Me. Don't get me wrong, I'll still probably end up eating one of them, but they're pretty gross.

The first minion started to run towards *Stringbing* who was busy trying to unwrap our principal. But because she was watching him, she never saw the second one leap into the air. And the worst part is that none of us warned her. I don't know why, we just didn't. Some team *we* are!

He landed right on top of her. *Splat!* Then the other one jumped on too. *Splat!* We watched, waiting to see what happened to Kimmy. I know it's bad. If this had happened two weeks ago, we would have been happy to see her attacked by giant meatloaf monsters. But, she's actually kind of grown on us. Like a rash. But a nice rash.

Miss Mary cackled, meaning she laughed *sorta* like a witch again. All of a sudden we saw something slide from under them. It was *Stringbing*, I guess you can't flatten someone who is already flat as a pancake. Man, I *gotta* stop thinking about pancakes!

"*Stringbing*, move!" yelled *Knowitall*.

"*KK*," she says.

No-No (I think that's what I'll call *Knowitall*) leaned his pimply face forward and squinted his eyes. A yellow beam shot out from his big nerdy glasses. "Let's see how you monsters like my Opti-Beam," he said. Uh-oh, here it comes.

187

"Opti is a prefix that means …"

"We know already!" snapped *Stringbing*.

"*Beaverine*, time to cut the meatloaf!" he added.

"Better than having to cut the cheese!" said *Beav*. "Now *that's* funny!"

"No it's not!" yelled *No-No*.

Okay, maybe that one was a little funny. But I make sure not to laugh *'cause* it will only encourage him.

Besides, I'm still too scared to laugh right now.

Beaverine ran over to the two meatloaf monsters who were still in a pile right next to the principal. *No-No's* Opti-Beam seemed to stun them. *Beav* opened his mouth wide exposing his two six-inch-long razor-sharp metal teeth.

CHOMP!

A big chunk of meatloaf flew into the air.

"Hungry? *Blubber Boy*?" *No-No* asked, looking at me.

"Always!" I said. And I'm not lying either, I told you, I really am *always* hungry!

"Bon appetite!" he said.

"Now *that's* French!" added *Stringbing*.

So that's what I did. I ate it. When I'm big like this, I can eat almost anything. And it all tastes good, no matter what it is. Once I ate a phone book. You know, I don't know why I keep telling you stuff like that. But I guess better you than Kimmy. She'd post it on her stupid blog, then the whole school would know my secrets. That's foul! When the first minion was gone, *Beav* began slicing up the other one, and I ate 'im as fast as he could slice 'im.

"Really?" *Beaverine* asked while looking at me as I polished off the last piece of the second minion. I guess he was shocked at what I just did. Shoot, I'd be shocked too if I wasn't already used to doing what I do.

"No ketchup, no nothing, just *chomp chomp chomp*?" he added.

"Just *chomp chomp chomp*," I answered wiping my chin with my sleeve. Then I stopped to watch the stain on my sleeve disappear. They may look strange, but these uniforms *do* have some cool features.

"My minions!" said Miss Mary. "You leave them alone." Suddenly she reached into her apron and pulled out a handful of something else and screamed in that foreign language again.

"Uh-oh, watch out, she's speaking French again," said *Beav*.

"*OMG*, I told you, that's *not* French!" snapped *Stringy*. I don't think she knows how to speak in a normal tone. She's either quiet, which is rare, or she's yelling, which is often.

"Well how do you know, *Stringbing*?"

"I told you I know French," she snapped again. "When I turn 18, I'm going to move to Paris and start my own fashion line."

"What are you going to call it, FAT Farm?" said *Beaverine* cracking himself up. "And I mean F-A-T, not P-H-A-T!"

Stringbing stopped short and started blinking and rubbing her eyes like crazy. After a few seconds, she looked at *Beaverine*. And not just any look, the look of death! He put his hands up like you do when you know you're about to get hit.

"Wait, *Stringbing*, I forgot, I'm sorry!" he says.

"Well I've got news for you, *Mister Comedian*, you make people laugh all right, but *no one* is laughing *with* you, we're all laughing *at* you!"

Beaverine put his hand over his mouth and scrunched up his face like he just bit his tongue. "*C'mon*, now! You didn't have to do that, I *said* I was sorry!" he screamed. His voice cracked a little like he was about to cry.

"Well you're sorry now!" snarled *Stringbing*.

I know he started it, but I still feel bad for him. See? That's another big difference between boys and girls — Boys insult you based on what they think is funny. Even if it's stupid like calling someone a *poopie-head*. Like his joke about Fat Farm, instead of Phat Farm. But it wasn't so much that Kimmy, I mean *Stringbing*, is fat in real life (she is, which made it even funnier), but it was that it was a clever pun. But girls? ... Shoot, when girls insult you they go right for the heart. "You're poor," "you're adopted," "nobody likes you," "you've got zits." That's why I *never* pick on girls. *Never!* I'd rather pick on the biggest boy in school than the smallest girl! Trust me!

I didn't really know what "alter your molecular structure to super dense" meant, but I was guessing that he meant to make myself super heavy. So I did! And I flattened that monster like a pancake. *Mmmm* … I could really go for some pancakes right now. Butter … real maple syrup … Oh sorry, where was I? Oh yeah, while *No-No* was screaming at *Beav* and *Stringbing* for always arguing, he lost his own focus.

Miss Mary threw something in his direction. But just as it was about to hit him, *Mini* pops up out of nowhere and pushes him out of the way. Then she shrinks back down and disappears into the grass again. I have to admit, that was pretty cool.

"Just look at what almost happened!" yelled *Knowitall*. "Your stupid arguing almost got me seriously hurt! We're a team, so let's start acting like one!"

"Sorry, dude," says *Beav*. *Stringbing* also said something, but it was in French. It was probably "sorry" also, but she couldn't just say it in English like a normal person. She needs to show the world that she really *does* know French. I wonder if Miss Mary would want to join our team instead of Kimmy? Or maybe even one of those meatloaf dudes. Anyone! Actually a meatloaf dude would be cool 'cause if I ever got hungry in the middle of a fight, I could just take a bite of him. *Mmmmmm* meatloaf …

We all take a minute to catch our breath and see where everyone is. Me, the *Beav*, *Stringy* and *No-No* all line up in front of our principal, who's still wiggling like a worm trying to break free. I guess *Mini* is still in the grass somewhere waiting to pop up again. Hope she doesn't get eaten by a squirrel. Miss Mary was now floating in the middle circle of the school's driveway, right in front of the flagpole.

I look over at Principal Marshand. He saw me looking and gave me a wink. That must mean he's happy with what we're doing so far. Or maybe he's just glad that we're not all dead yet. Then again, he could just have meatloaf in his eye.

Miss Mary looked at us and said, "Here, kids. Have a ball. A meatball!" She flung her arm forward and we see them coming at us. First they were small, then they got big. When the first one was about to hit me, my soccer instincts kicked in and I slammed it with my foot like I was in the middle of a penalty kick. The meatball slammed into one of the other ones that she threw at us. I'll eat them in a minute, but first I need to take care of another meatball that's heading my way. Right when it's about to hit me, I spin around, hop in the air, and get ready for my epic bicycle kick (That's when I turn backwards and kick the ball over my head). I won a game for our school a few weeks back. So here it goes, spin, jump and ...

SLAM!!!

But the slam everyone heard, wasn't me kicking the meatball. It was me falling flat on my back. How could I be so stupid? Of course I can't jump anymore, I weigh 300 pounds!!! The meatball sails past me and rolls off. My problem is now that I'm on my back, how am I ever going to get back up? These powers just get worse and worse!

The jerks behind the cars busted out laughing. My underwear felt like it went so far up my butt that it probably rubbed up against my lungs! Even Miss Mary actually laughed. "*Didja* see the way the little fat boy bounced when he hit the ground? Poor baby. That's a shame that someone his age can be so fat. You're not too young to get diabetes, you know."

"I've fallen and I can't get up," yells one of the kids in the crowd. How humiliating. Who laughs at someone just because they fell down? Just then, my brain started flashing images inside my head like I was watching a movie. And it was mostly of me laughing at kids falling down and getting hurt. But this time I can see the sadness on their faces ... their frowns ... their sad eyes ... their tears ... *dag*.

"I've cooked up some more special treats for you thankless kids today. Don't worry, they won't hurt a bit. Let's start with some *black-eyed peas!*" She reached into her pouch again and tossed a hand full of something at the others. And all I could do was lay there like a turtle on its back.

"Technically, Miss Mary, black-eyed peas are actually more of a bean than a pea. They've been a staple in the Southern diet for over 300 years." Guess who said that? Yep, *Knowitall*. You know, when you first meet him, he seems really annoying because he's always showing off how smart he is. Then, when you're around him a bit, you get used to him. Then after a while, he gets even more annoying. In fact, if I had her exploding peas or beans, I'd blow him up myself!

The peas exploded into little clouds of smoke. Hey, these black-eyed-peas don't seem bad. Not bad at all. Except when my Uncle Ed eats them, but that's a whole '*nother* story. These were like little grenades.

I saw *Mini* dodging and weaving to avoid the clouds. But *Stringbing* wasn't so lucky. One of the beans exploded pretty close to her. Didn't seem to do much at all. Then all of a sudden she just keeled over like she fell fast asleep. Then Miss Mary shot the spaghetti stuff and wrapped her up like the principal.

"It's knock out gas!" yelled *Knowitall*.

Yep, just like when Uncle Ed eats them. You don't *wanna* be around HIS knock out gas either! Trust me on that one.

Then Miss Mary turned towards *Beaverine*. "Hold still!" she snarled.

"No thanks," said *Beaverine*, "the only black-eyed-peas I like is the singing group. And I don't even like *all* their songs."

"Here, Miss Mary, let's see how you like my Opti-Beam."

ZZAAAPPP!!!

The blast hit her hand and sent the rest of the beans flying. They exploded all around her giving her quite a jolt. But unfortunately, the gas had no effect on her.

"Well, I'm glad your goofy glasses do something besides make you look silly," said Miss Mary. *Knowitall* flinched. He must have just gotten one of those brain freezes. And the thing is, we have to pretend like it doesn't hurt. Just walk it off. Because if people knew how their words hurt us, they'd insult us all the time.

Miss Mary reached to her side and grabbed the ladle from her belt. I think it's called a ladle. That's one of those big scoopy things that you use to get soup out of the pot.

"Well if you won't stay still, maybe this will help!" she said as she flung the contents of the ladle. Out came this white paste that hit the *Beav* right on his legs. It didn't seem to hurt, but it hardened almost immediately, like cement. He was like a statue from the waste down. And he couldn't bend down to free himself with his teeth.

"And do you know the worst part is that stuff holding you down to the ground is made from the mashed potato mix they make me cook for you? It's a *cryin'* shame what they make me cook for you kids," said Miss Mary. "That's why so many of you are overweight. Your bodies can't digest this trash. Just look at the size of some of you!" she said pointing to me. "It's amazing they found a costume in your size."

"Ouch!"

"But now since you tried to stop me, you have to pay," she added. "Now who else wants mashed potatoes?"

"*Blubber Boy*, put your hand down!" *Knowitall* said yelling at me.

"I can't help it, I really do want mashed potatoes. All this talk about food is making me hungry!" I said in my defense.

She reached into her pouch and pulled out another handful of black-eyed peas.

"I'm sorry, sweetie, but Miss Mary can't let you *squash* her plans!... Even though I like squash. It's good for *ya*, it's got vitamins like A, B and calcium. But you all don't know nothing *'bout* vegetables, do *ya*? And when I make them, no one eats them. It hurts my heart to watch that much food go to waste. It's a sin! But let me make chicken nuggets and we run out every single time. Can't heat them up fast enough. Some of you kids just don't have home training, that's what's wrong! So now I have to teach *ya*."

I looked over at *Knowitall* who was now trying frantically to pull the spaghetti stuff off of Principal Marshand. He was screaming, "What am I supposed to do?! We need your help!"

He pulled as hard as he could and finally it started to move a bit. "We can't beat her, she's too strong!" he said again.

He tugged one last time and pulled off a big chunk of the spaghetti that was covering Marshand's mouth.

"You can do it!" said Principal Marshand.

"But how? My body is so weak?!" he screamed back.

"Your body can *never* be as strong as your mind!" he said to Dex, I mean *Knowitall*.

"But I ... Wait a minute," I heard *Knowitall* say, like he just figured out the meaning of life. "She's not —"

But before he could finish his sentence, she raised up her arm and tossed more of those exploding peas at him. *Knowitall* used *Barney* to shoot most of them, but a few got through and exploded at his feet. He tried to hold his breath, but the cloud was too big. First he went down on one knee, then on all fours.

"*Mini*, be nice!" he said as he laid down and went to sleep. A loud laugh shot through the air. Miss Mary's, not *Knowitall's*.

195

"*No-No!*" I yell. But it was too late. He's out cold. "Be nice?" What the heck did he mean by that? Who should Mina be nice to? Me? I know he didn't mean for us to be nice to Miss Mary. Maybe the gas made him crazy too.

Miss Mary starts to speak again, "Let's see what else I can *whip up*. *Pound* cake? … Or maybe a nice glass of *punch*? That boy with the buck teeth isn't the only one who's clever, you know?"

"I'd like some pound cake!" I said, without missing a beat. Okay, I admit it, *I have a serious problem*! Even *you* know that nothing good can come of this, but I just couldn't help but say yes. "And some punch, too, please!"

"Boy, Miss Mary, I don't know who writes your material, but whoever it is, they're hired," says *Beaverine*. "*Black-eyed* peas, *pound* cake, *punch*, *squash* … That's some funny stuff! And if you made minions out of that spaghetti stuff, and they took over people's identities, you could call them *im-pastas*! Get it?"

I don't think she did, '*cause* she reached into her pouch and pulled out more peas. With the *Beav's* legs cemented to the ground, he was helpless. Another cloud of gas, and he was asleep too.

Well, since three of us are asleep, and I can't get back on my feet, I guess that means it's up to *Mini* … all six inches of her. We're doomed!

What made this worse is that even some of the kids who are watching are still laughing at us. They don't realize that if we fail, they'll be no one to save them.

"Hey, way to go, guys. We sure feel safe knowing that you and the *Fat-tastic* Four are here to protect us," yells one of the jerks.

Miss Mary looks around and sees no one moving but me. My arms and legs flailing like I'm some *sorta* insane upside-down swimmer. She reaches in her pouch again. Tosses something in my direction. It explodes into a little white cloud and I go to *sleeeeeee* …

38

LAST MOUSE STANDING

— by Mini Mouth

"Mini, be nice?!" What the heck does that mean? And the fact that he passed out right after he said it does me no good at all.

How do they expect me to fight our floating, green, psycho, head cook all alone while all of my teammates are out of commission? *Blubber Boy, Stringbing, Beaverine* and ol' smarty pants. So it's up to me. But what can I do when I'm only six-inches tall and no one can hear me talk?

"You kids, I'm *gonna* teach you all. Every last one of you! Do you know how long I've been at this school? I was here when some of your parents went here! And all I get are complaints. Nothing but complaints. Got them back then, still get them now. Do you know the last time someone looked me in the eye and said 'thank you?' Well, do you? … 1984! That's when! And I cook everyday for you. Then I serve you all. And for what? It's bad enough that you don't treat me with respect, but you don't even treat me like a human being sometimes!"

Wow, she has really lost it! And as soon as I thought it couldn't get any worse, she started to glow even brighter. I think her power might be tied to how angry she is. And right now, she's pretty angry. But how can I fight someone who is both bigger *and* stronger than me? And angrier than me? Right now she's probably the only person in school who I can't out-yell. And even if I could, no one can hear me because right now I can't yell. These aren't powers, they're a curse!!!

Miss Mary continued, "I tried to make healthy lunches for years, but the school board is always trying to cut corners. So I feed ya all crap. All *yous* want is chicken nuggets and french fries. Well I got news for *ya,* they don't even use real chicken to make those nuggets we buy! That's why you're all so unhealthy! There are 12 year olds with diabetes now because of these toxic diets. And you need to work harder to support me," she said while looking at Principal Marshand who was still on the ground wrapped up in spaghetti. But you knew that already, right?

Miss Mary started speaking Martian again. That's always a bad sign. What I wouldn't give to have *Beaverine* here, even if I *did* have to listen to his jokes. She raised her arms in the air and started to glow more than ever. Then all at once, the wind picked up like a scene from one of those movies where aliens are about to land or something. Then all of a sudden, the cafeteria doors blew wide open and stuff started flying through the windows. Food stuff!

"You kids want junk food? Here *ya* are! All the stuff I never wanted to feed you, but they make me. This is not stuff that young bodies need!"

There it was, a flying stream of chicken nuggets, fries, soda, cheese spread, hot dogs, nachos ... a junk food lover's dream; all flying out of our cafeteria and swirling around like a tornado. Then it started to form into something. Something big. Even bigger than the meatloaf minions! Then it took shape. The shape ... of a monster! *Yikes!!!* It must be about 30-feet tall. Now the expression on Miss Mary's face was pure anger. The monster started to move. *BOOM! BOOM! BOOM!* That's how its footsteps shook the ground.

And after all that happened today, do you believe there are still kids standing around watching? Suddenly, the monster reaches behind one of the cars and snatched up two of the kids who were hiding. They were the same kids who were making fun of how fat Bobby is.

And now it's opening its mouth to eat them, and there is nothing I can do! Nothing!!! Then stuff started shooting out of its mouth and covered the two boys. Wait, it wasn't eating them, it was feeding them! Like how a mother bird feeds its babies. Gross! And before my eyes, they started to plump up, just like *Blubber Boy!* Gross!

Sure *now* the others finally get a clue and start to run. But this thing is big. It catches up to them after only two steps. One by one, it picks them up, opens its mouth and sprays them like it did to the others. And you guessed it, they plumped up too. At this rate we're going to have a whole school full of *Blubber Boys* and girls! Even worse than how it is now!

Then who do I see running for her life? Meagan Stevens!!! You all remember her, she's my enemy from four-square. Oh, this is *gonna* be good. I can't wait to see her get all plumped up like the other kids.

But then, instead of me sitting back and enjoying the show. Something happened. *FFFT!*

I changed back into my normal self.

So now, instead of being safe while hiding in the grass, there I was, in the middle of the all the action as Mina Madsen!!! I was big again. Oh no!

"Well, where did you come from?" asked Miss Mary. Let's see what I have for you!

Uh-oh. Without being small or fast, I'm a sitting duck. So I kicked off my flip-flops and started running. Not as fast as when I'm *Mini Mouth*, but as fast as I could go. I looked over at the rest of the guys to see if they had changed back too, but they hadn't. Why just me?

Before I knew it, I was right near Meagan. The food monster-thingy was closing in on her. Luckily it's not as fast as those meatloaf things. Then Meagan falls down. Wouldn't you know it? Just like in those movies. Why do the stupid people always fall down? How hard is it to run? We've been running our whole lives! Now that I see the look of fear on her face, I can't just watch and let that thing grab her … as much as I'd like to.

There's no way I can get to her in time. Just then, I see the meatball that Bobby tried to soccer kick. I run over and swoop it up in one motion. The monster reaches out its hand to pick her up.

"Here's the rules," I say while cocking back my arm, "no body parts, no chicken feet, and most of all, no more making kids fat!!!" Then I toss the meatball up and punch it with my fist as hard as I can. Which is pretty hard! It slammed into the monster's arm causing an explosion of hot dogs and snapping it off at the elbow. SCORE! Then I ran over to Meagan who's still on the ground screaming like a baby and hold out my hand. "Come with me if you want to live," I say. Sorry, but my dad just watched all the Terminator movies last weekend, and that was one of the lines I kept hearing over and over.

"Mina?" she says, looking at me.

"Come on, get up!!!" I yell. "That thing is almost on top of us! Come on!!!"

Finally she gives me her hand. I help her up then look around to see the monster's other gigantic hand reaching down to grab us. I yanked her out of the way and we both stumbled forward. I felt the breeze from its hand as it swooped by us. Boy, that was close!

"Now, go ahead, get out of here!" I yelled at her.

She took a few steps forward then stopped. But before she turned around …

FFFFT!

I changed back into *Mini Mouth*!

"Mina?" said Meagan. "Mina, where did you go? Thank you, Mina, wherever you are."

I hid in the grass so she didn't see me. Why won't she leave already?

Then when she realized that the monster was still there, she turned and ran. *Whew!* Luckily she's not as dumb as I thought. But now that I'm back to being small, what do I do to stop Miss Mary? What can I do?

"There! Is that what you want?" screamed Miss Mary. "Childhood obesity? Diabetes? I tried to feed you vegetables!!!"

Wait a minute. "I tried to feed you vegetables?" That's not a bad thing to say. Then I started to remember some of the other things that she said to us today. "This is not the stuff that young bodies need." — "I'm *gonna* teach you a lesson. One that if you don't learn, it'll hurt ya!" Wait, she didn't say that SHE would hurt us, she was talking about the crappy food! All day she's been talking about how we won't eat the things that she considers to be good food, and how they make her feed us garbage. Maybe *she's* the one who's hurt. You know, *like*, her feelings, not her body. Wow, I can't believe I just said that. I sound like my mom. Is it possible that Miss Mary actually *cares* about us? *Omigosh*, maybe that's what Knowitall meant when he said to "be nice." He meant to be nice to Miss Mary … I hope.

Only one way to find out. It's a gamble, but I don't know what else to do. I ran towards Miss Mary as fast as I could. She doesn't see me coming because I'm still hiding in the grass. Then when I get to her, I leap as high as I can and latch on to the end of her untied shoe lace. I pull myself up and start to climb until I got up to her shoulders.

I can't believe I'm up here and she doesn't feel me. *Eww*, she could probably stand to have some of these ear hairs plucked. *Oooh gosh*, now I sound like Kimmy! I wish *Knowitall* was here to help me. I look over to see the monster chasing kids around the four-square court. Luckily Meagan had the sense to keep running. If I don't stop that thing now, the thinnest person in the school will be Kimmy. Here it goes. Me being nice!

"Miss Mary, I'm sorry!" I whispered in her ear.

"What, who said that?" she asked stunned.

"I'm really sorry that we always make fun of your cooking. And I know you try to make good things for us to eat, but, *like*, we'd rather eat junk."

"You sure do."

"Yeah, and you know what else? I really like your meatloaf, Miss Mary.

I really do."

"Really? … It's my mother's recipe. The secret is chopped onions and just a touch of fresh horseradish."

"What's horseradish?"

"It's a root. The stuff that gives cocktail sauce its zing. Plus it's high in Vitamin C and so many other things. I just love it."

"Really? I love shrimp cocktail, Miss Mary. And I like the salads you make with the sunflower seeds and the little red jelly things. I put some on my plate every day. I wish my mom did that, but she makes us a lot of microwave stuff 'cause she's always working."

"No, I don't use no microwave, child. Don't trust it. And that's not jelly, those are pomegranate seeds. I can't believe you noticed."

"Yep. Boy, Miss Mary you really know how to cook, don't you?"

"You're darn right I do. I studied at the Culinary Institute. My daddy even spent his life's savings to send me to Paris to learn from the Masters. But when I came back to America, I couldn't get a job. No one would hire me 'cause they didn't hire colored folks for good jobs back then. Not as a cook anyway. Oh I could have gotten plenty of work as a cleaning lady. But *I am a chef!!! I can even speak French! Je suis un chef fantastique!**"

"I believe you, Miss Mary. Maybe I can talk to the headmaster about having you teach a cooking class here or something. Would you like that?"

"Really? You'd do that for me? And you really like my meatloaf? You ain't just saying that? And I don't *wanna* make no more of those Sloppy Joes. I want to make something healthier. The school board tells me what to make, but I want to be able to create my own menu."

"No, Miss Mary, I'm not just saying that. I really will try to help you. My mom is a lawyer. I'll get her to help too. And she's good and mean!"

"And you know my name. No one ever refers to me by my name. It's always just 'hey you.' Some of these kids are so rude. Then their parents come and they're just as bad. That's nice that someone wants to help. Thank you, sweetheart, wherever you are. I may not be able to see, you, but Miss Mary hears you loud and clear."

Suddenly I heard a big thump. It was the junk food monster. It started to fall apart. It's like the glue that was holding it together stopped working. Finally it fell flat on its face and busted apart like a meat-filled piñata. I

* I am a fantastic chef!

know, that sounds gross. There was junk food everywhere. Maybe, *like*, she couldn't focus on keeping it together and talk to me at the same time. Or maybe she just didn't want to keep it together anymore. Whatever the reason, it's working. I have to keep her talking.

"My mom said that one time you tried to stop serving us pizza for lunch. But I have to admit, Miss Mary, when I heard that, I thought you were doing that to punish us. But you just wanted us to eat better, didn't you?"

"Yes, *baby*, Miss Mary only wanted to look out for you. But do you know that the school district has pizza listed as a healthy food 'cause it's got tomato sauce on it? And they consider tomatoes a vegetables. Or fruit, I forget which one. And you eat too many darn french fries too. I try to limit how much fried food you all eat. Sugar, high fructose corn syrup … And those blasted mashed potatoes are like cement. Do you see what it did to that red-headed boy with the big teeth? I stuck him right to the ground. Didn't hurt him though. But, if he don't need to go to a dentist, I don't know who does."

"Yeah, I'll tell him."

Well I didn't understand everything she said like the '*frotos syrup*' or whatever, but it sounded like it made sense. I never knew she was so smart. Suddenly, I felt a thud. It was Miss Mary landing on the ground. She wasn't floating anymore. I moved to the very edge of her shoulder to take a look at her. And you know what? She wasn't so green anymore either. In fact, her skin was going back to its natural color of toasted brown sugar. The same as mine. Well at least how mine is when I change. It was beautiful.

"Well thank you, baby. No one ever took the time to say anything nice to me. Not here anyway."

"You're welcome, Miss Mary. I'm just sorry I didn't do it sooner."

"Miss Mary is tired now, honey. I have to go sit down."

I crawled down off her shoulder and hopped back in the grass. She turned to look to see who I was, but still couldn't see me.

"Thank you, baby," she said, and for the first time ever, I saw her smile.

As she walked towards the bench in the middle of the circle, I heard her humming a song. Weird. Wonder if she ever did that before and I just never noticed. Guess I'm one of those disrespectful brats that she was talking about. Here's a lady that serves me food every school day and I've never once said anything nice to her. In fact, I don't think I ever said anything to her. Not even *thank you*.

What a loser I am!

One by one, my super-powered teammates started to wake up. First was Dex, then Kimmy, then Buck. I freed Buck first so he could use his sharp teeth to cut Principal Marshand and Kimmy out of that spaghetti. Then we all had to work together to help Bobby stand up. Boy, it was like picking up Humpty Dumpty.

The principal was very formal with us while the other kids were around, I guess he was pretending that he didn't know us to keep our identities a secret.

"I'd like to thank you all for your help," he said.

"No problem," I said while growing as big as I can. When I'm in uniform that only seems to be about 12 inches tall. And I can shrink down to about as small as four inches.

"I'm going to check on Miss Mary to make sure she's all right. I'll run some tests on her to make sure that she's back to normal. Then I have to figure out how she got ahold of the Orb. Obviously between her and you guys, I have to increase my security."

"Well let's hope she doesn't go completely back to normal," said Buck.

"Hey, she's not that bad when you give her a chance," I said. Wow, who *am* I? I can't believe I just said that.

"No, she's not," added the principal. "And she's right, I need to fight for her to improve our menu ... You kids should head home in case the police arrive. I don't know how we're going to explain all of this."

Just then we heard a cheer. It was a bunch of fifth graders running towards the fallen monster. Picking up hot dogs and chicken nuggets like it was the happiest, crappiest Thanksgiving ever. Pretty disgusting if you ask me. I hope Miss Mary didn't see this, that's enough to turn *anyone* green!"

"Hey, stop eating that junk," yelled the principal. "*Hmmm,* I also have to find a way to turn those kids back to their normal size. They look like you, *Blubber Boy ... Blubber Boy?* Hey, where'd he go?"

You guessed it. Right in the middle of all the junk-food eating kids.

They stopped when they saw him. But once he started eating, they all joined right in. Something tells me there's not going to be a lot to clean up.

"I'll also have to call these kids' parents and tell them that sports practice ended late. That will give me more time to figure out how to get these kids back to normal. *Hmmm,* I wonder if I can zap their memories? You guys need to change back to normal so you can go home. But before you go, I just want you to know how thankful I am for your help, and what a great job you did."

And on that note, we all went back to the hideout so we could turn back into our normal selves without being seen. We had to drag Bobby away from the food. He grabbed a couple of hot dogs to eat on the way. If we thought that last week was weird, then today has got to be a thousand times weirder!

1 OUT 10 STUDENTS DROP OUT OF SCHOOL BECAUSE OF REPEATED BULLYING.
— DoSomething.org

39

THE OFFENDERS

— by Mini Mouth

"So let me get this right …" said *Beaverine* "… after all that fighting we did, you beat her with *words*? And not even bad words, you defeated her by talking *nice*?!"

"Yeah, that was the last thing that *Knowitall* said before he fell out. I didn't know what else to do. We sure weren't getting anywhere by trying to fight her with force. And I would have asked you guys for suggestions, but you were too busy taking a *nappy-poo.*"

"Oh, now *you've* got jokes, huh, Mina?" said Dex.

"Well, maybe a few," I said.

"So, let me get this right, Miss Mary was really *good*?"

"Well, she didn't do anything to hurt us, did she? I mean, she stuck us to the ground. She put us to sleep …"

"But she tried to hit me with a meatball! And what about that giant monster?"

"Well, maybe she was trying to get all the junk food out of our cafeteria," I said.

"Then she could have just cooked it all, we would have been glad to eat it."

"But that's the point, she didn't *want* us to eat it. I just feel bad for her. Miss Mary is one of those folks who seems like nothing good has ever happened to her in her whole life. Including working here," I said.

"Well, all I can say is I know it's *gonna* be a *looonnnggg* time before I can ever eat meatloaf or black-eyed-peas again," said Bobby. "At least not until the next time I change into *Blubber Boy*, 'cause then I'll eat *anything*!"

"Well at least it was meatloaf, 'cause if those minions had been made of Sloppy Joes, I think we'd all be dead now," added Kimmy.

"You can say that again!"

"So, *like*, what do we do now? I mean with these powers?"

"Well, that's up to you," said Principal Marshand, who once again entered the room without anyone hearing him. "I still don't know how long you will have them."

"I guess that means that we should enjoy them while they last."

"Enjoy them? Who says I *enjoy* being as flat as a pancake? And now

do I have to go around risking my life and doing good deeds for people for the rest of my life? And then everytime I try to use them for something selfish or for revenge, which is what I'd rather do, they stop working?" asked an upset Kimmy.

Hey, that's what happened to me! When I didn't want to help Meagan, they stopped working. Just then, I heard Principal Marshand's voice pop into my head. I remember when he told us how sitting around and doing nothing is almost as bad as the one who does the bad thing to begin with.

"Oh no, that dumb orb is *forcing* us to do the right thing!!!" I yelled.

"Well, yes, that would appear to be the case, Miss Madsen. But I think you should all begin by deciding if these abilities are a blessing or a curse."

"*Curse!!!*" we all said at the same time.

"Uh-uh-uh-uh," said the principal while making that *shushing* gesture with his finger. "I don't want to know now, sleep on it and let me know in detention tomorrow."

"Wait a minute, *bro*, you *tellin'* me that we just saved the school from being destroyed and we STILL *gotta* serve detention? *'sta loco!*"

"*You* didn't save the school, *Knowitall, Blubber Boy, Mini Mouth, Stringbing* and *Beaverine* did. But as far as the school goes, Dex, Bobby, Mina, Kimmy and Buck are still bullies who have a *lot* of work to do, and a lot of fences to mend. In fact, it's time I address the bullying problem in this school head on. I think we need to have a speaker come and address the assembly."

"Sigh!" we all said while making a variety of sounds like sucking our teeth and blowing our breath.

"Well, time to go, I have to get back to the kids. I think I've figured out a way to return them back to their normal size. And I can take away a bit of their memories using one of the tools the *Orderan* used on our criminals. I've had to do it to a few of the board members occasionally. Just never had to do it to so many people at once before. The kids are all gathering in the auditorium as we speak. Thank you for your help again, I couldn't have done it without you. Now all that's left is to figure out how Miss Mary got ahold of the orb. The strange thing was that after you found it, I made it even more secure. I'm not sure how she could have gotten to it."

"Could there be another one?" we asked.

"Well, our ship was equipped with a few, but after the crash, I never saw them again. I just assumed they were destroyed. And it's doubtful that after all of these years one could have been on school property without me knowing about it. I'll have to process that. Well, I guess I'd better go. Let yourselves out."

We said goodbye to Principal Marshand, then stood around and talked for a while. We recapped the fight blow by blow, each giving his, or her, own point of view.

"Yo, Bobby," said Buck.

"What?"

"Well, when you were like *'I've fallen and I can't get up,'* why didn't you just change back to yourself, stand up, then change back to *Blubber Boy*?

"And let everyone know that that fat superhero is ME? No way. I'd stay there all night if I had to, dude."

After about 20 minutes, we all headed upstairs to meet our parents. Principal M. closed the main entrance so all our folks had to go around to the back where there was no mess. Luckily he had also sent out a message to everyone who was coming to pick us up, that they should come at 4:30 instead of 4:00. It was time to go.

"Bye, dudes."

"Ciao."

"Adios, *bros*."

"Aw-ight, dudes."

"*Like*, see ya later."

We headed outside to catch our rides before our Martian principal decide that he wanted to try to zap *our* memories too. Just in case.

This was, *like*, the weirdest day ever!

EPILOGUE

"That's an ending ..."

"They know, Dex. This is probably not the only book they've ever read, you know."

MINA aka MINI MOUTH

Dad was still a little late today. Went to pick up Joy first today, she had music practice and it went long. Did I tell you we're twins but we don't go to the same school? She goes to one that is more for kids with musical or artistic talents. She plays the cello.

We went home and did all the things we always did. But for some reason it was different. I tried to look at them with "new eyes" just like I did with Miss Mary, hoping I would find something different. I didn't talk much, just tried to study them like I was meeting them for the first time.

My dad seems a bit like he's scared. I think maybe the reason why he's always on the phone is because he wants us to see how hard he's looking for a job. I wonder if he really is, or if he just wants us to *think* he is.

My mom talks on the phone a lot too, but maybe hers is to show how much more she has to do since she's paying all the bills. That's why she doesn't buy anything for dinner that she can't zap in the microwave for a few minutes.

And Joy. I really didn't see anything all that bad about her. She's my twin sister, but when I looked at myself in the mirror, I've done everything I can *not* to look anything like her. My clothes, my hair ... for two kids who *kinda* look alike, we look *nothing* alike. I never noticed that before.

As I got into bed, I thought a lot about that. I put the light back on, reached under my pillow and went out into the hallway. I knocked on Joy's door. "Come in," she said.

"Um ... Joy?"

"Mina, is that you? Are you okay?"

"Yeah, I'm fine. I just wanted you to know that ... that ... well, here..."

"My necklace!!! *You found it!* Oh thank you, thank you, thank you! I thought I would never see it again! Oh, Mina, where on Earth was it?"

"Around, you know, I don't remember exactly," I said. I didn't know what else to say after that. I just *kinda* stared at the stupid Justin Bieber poster over her bed. And I really *hate* Justin Bieber. Luckily she's got one of a couple of cats too, so I decided to look at that one instead. It was either that, or look at Hairball who was laying at the foot of her bed. I chose the poster.

"Hey, you got a new ring," she said to me.

"No, it's the same one I always wear."

"But, Mina, this one is bright blue, the one you always wear is black."

"That's weird. But I swear it's the same one. Trust me."

"Hey, Mina, this must be one of the mood rings that we got at that fair when we were little. Remember?"

"Oh, yeah. Now I remember. It's a mood ring? But wait … you mean … oh nevermind … But it's been black for, *like*, a year. Why did it change colors *now*? *Hmmmm …*"

That's *gonna* keep me up tonight.

"Well … good night, Joy" I said as I turned and walked away.

"Mina?"

"Yeah, Joy?"

"You *wanna* sit down? Maybe we could talk for a while?"

"Um, *nah*, maybe some other time, I had a pretty long day," I said while nervously twisting my friendship bracelet around my wrist.

"Okay, well thanks again. Nitey nite, don't let the bed bugs bite," she sang. I have to admit, that was still kind of annoying.

"Okay, I'll try not to let myself be bitten by parasites."

"And, Mina?"

"YES, JOY?"

"Snowball says goodnight too."

"Good night, Hairball."

"*Snowball!*" she corrected.

Oops, I really didn't mean to do that on purpose. I guess I've done it on purpose so often that it just *kinda* slipped out.

I went back to my room and snuggled up with Chauncey (that's my Teddy bear, remember?). I let out a big sigh, like I had been holding my breath for a year. Then I went off to sleep.

DEX aka KNOWITALL

Didn't feel like going to the skate park today. Instead I went straight home. I really just wanted to see my family. I opened the door and got my whiff of food cooking. I could use a routine after today. And there was Abuela, there to greet me with a hug. And I hugged her back just as tight. She smiled. I love her smile, it makes her face light up like a flashlight. I put my shades by the door, then washed my hands and sat down at the table to wait for everyone else. Talked to Abuela in Spanish a bit. I zoned out a bit, and when I got my focus back, I caught myself *boppin'* my head back and forth to the music that was playing. Then it hit me, that wasn't a radio or a CD. It was my sister singing! Ugh, *Paula Ab-Ghoul* herself, *trying* yet again to sing.

Then I stopped and listened some more. You know, actually, if I had to admit it … today, for some reason, she didn't sound too bad.

'sta loco!!!

BUCK aka BEAVERINE

Wow, this was an amazing day. Everything is different. I know I am. I got off the bus and ran to the front door. For some reason I couldn't wait to get home. Maybe things will be different here too. As I hit the top step, the door swung wide open. It was Tammy. And she was smiling. And there was no sound of arguing in the background. Maybe today would be the start of something new. But as I walked through the door I felt a jolt. I was being tackled by Trina. They rolled me on my stomach then two of them, and I don't know which ones 'cause I couldn't see, sat on me while the other one began to pull off my sneakers and socks. I curled up my toes waiting to be tickled. But instead, I heard a sound like "sssssssssss." Then I felt something wet on the bottom of my feet. Next thing I know, my *three-big-mouthed-evil-sisters* get up and run towards the staircase. I get up and run after them. They're gonna get it. Man, what I wouldn't give to turn into *Beaverine* and just start chomping! They turn to run up the stairs. I turn to run up the stairs. They go UP the stairs. I slide PAST the stairs all the way into the dining room and fall over one of the dining room chairs. It, and I, flip over onto the floor. I hear something roll on the floor towards me. It doesn't stop until it *bonks* me on the head. I turn over and look at it. It's a can of *Pam!* You know, that spray cooking oil that you use on pots so food doesn't stick? That's what they sprayed on the bottom of my feet.

They run up the stairs laughing.

All I could think of is, compared to my *three-big-mouthed-evil-sisters*, I even miss the Meatloaf Minions!

KIMMY aka STRINGBING

"Hi, honey" said my mom. The school sent out a text telling all the parents to come later. Did something happen?"

"Oh, the field hockey game went in to double overtime, so we all went down to cheer for the team," I said.

"Oh, what a great show of support. Did they win?"

"Win what?" I asked.

"The field hockey game. The one that went into double overtime."

"Oh that, yes, we won 35-21."

"You mean your team scored 35 goals? That must be some sort of record!"

See, this is why I usually don't lie about stuff I don't know about, like sports. If you're going to lie, then do it about something that you know well. Like me and fashion. I try to change the subject before I look even more stupid.

"Thanks for coming to pick me up, Mommy."

"You're welcome, sweetie. But until we get a place to live, it's not like you can take the bus home. I tried to park in the corner so you wouldn't have to be seen in the minivan."

I felt a twinge when she said that. Not like the stuff that happens when someone insults me, but this one was more normal. I think what she said made me feel guilty.

"Since I had an extra half hour, I went to the market so you wouldn't have to go. I know how you hate to go grocery shopping. I brought you a sandwich. Honey roasted turkey!!!"

"*Yum!*" I tore into that sandwich like I was *Blubber Boy*. After about 15 minutes of silence, mom turned and looked at me.

"You're awfully quiet, did I park too close to your building? Did your friends see the van? I'm really sorry if they did."

Wow, I can't believe how awful hearing that made me feel. It was like the whole thing that Mina was saying about Miss Mary. How all we do is give her grief. It's bad enough to be a part of *that*, but then I think about what I've done to my own mom! And *no one* treats me better than her. Especially not my dad. And I make her park further from the school so she doesn't embarrass me. So SHE doesn't embarrass ME! Wow ... I stink!

"Kimmy, are you crying, what happened, did you get hurt?"

"I'm ... sniff ... sniff ... okay, Mommy ... I'll ... huff ... huff ... be fine."

She pulled over to the side and stopped the car. "Aw, baby, what's wrong?"

"Mom, dad left us and you have to go back to work, and we live in our van, and you work so hard, and all you do is try to make me happy and I'm just so ... so ..."

"Ungrateful?" she asked.

"Hey!" I said. "I'm not ungrateful!"

"I'm sorry, baby, then why are you crying?"

"Well, maybe I am. Just a little ... Okay, a *lot!* I'm really sorry, Mommy. And I'm sorry that daddy left you and you have to take care of me all by yourself now."

"Kimmy, taking care of you is the best part of my life."

Aw, now I feel even worse. "Well, I'll try to appreciate you more, Mommy, okay?"

"Well, I'm not going to lie, that would be nice," she said. "So how about some gelato? That always makes you happy."

"Yeah, but you like ice cream better. Maple walnut."

"That's true, maple walnut *is* my favorite."

"Then let's do *that*. Let's do something that *you* want to do for a change."

"Thank you, Kimmy. That would mean a lot."

"And it would mean a lot to me, too, Mommy."

BOBBY aka BLUBBER BOY

The most amazing thing that has ever happened just took place, and all that I can think about is whether or not I'm a bully. I mean, I can't be, right? I'm a nice guy. I treat my mom and my sisters good, I get good grades...

But, man, being fat, just for an hour, gave me a little taste of what that's like. And I hated it. Now I keep hearing Principal Marshand talking about "intent versus impact." It's starting to make more sense. Man, I know what a jerk my brother Bryce is to me, and it *kinda* makes me sad to think that I could be somebody's Bryce. So what he's saying is that even if I don't mean to be that bad, if that's how Reggie takes it, then it's the same thing.

And the worst part is that I can't even tell Reggie that I'm sorry 'cause he hasn't been to school all week. I hope he's sick. I mean, I don't hope that he's really sick, I just mean that I hope the reason he's not in school is because he's sick, not that he's afraid of me.

But I'm not a bully! Bullies are tough guys with tattoos. They beat up people and take their money. I don't do that. I was just having a little fun, that's all. So that makes it okay, right?

CLIFFHANGER

THE NEW PLAN

— by ?

It was a wasted effort. But now that I've seen what our orbs can do to humans, I can experiment on them until I get the results that I want. Miss Mary was just a start, but that didn't go quite the way I wanted. Obviously there was a lot more good in the old woman than I thought. But if *Gerolk* has super-powered children to do his bidding, then I must have the same.

I WILL have the same!

I just have to find the right combination. But why did he choose children? Maybe there's something in their youthful bodies that allows the orb to manipulate them more efficiently. Something that, since they are still growing, their bodies are more receptive of the orb's power. Ah, just who I was looking for.

"Mama, there's a man coming up the *dwiveway*. Mama?"

"Hello, young man," I said in a calming tone.

"Mama says I'm not *a-wowed* to talk to strangers."

"But I'm not a stranger, Reggie. I know all about you. You see, I'm the new head of school over at Nimoy Academy. And I'd like to talk to your mom about you transferring."

"But I *wike* my school."

"Do you? Do you really? You mean you like getting picked on day after day? You like having people call you names? Pulling your underwear up out of your pants? Teasing you about the way you speak? You *really* like that?"

"Well, no. No. Not *weally.*"

"Then what would you say if I told you that I could give you the power to change your life? To make you powerful. And with this power, you would be able to get back at all the kids who have made you feel so bad for so long? What would you say to that?" I asked.

"Hello, may I help you, sir? ... Reggie, go in the house," said his mother who came out of the house to check on her son.

"I'm sorry, ma'am, I know you've taught him not to speak to strangers, but I was actually looking for you. I'd like to talk to you about a new school for Reggie."

"And who are you, may I ask?"

"I am Headmaster Gregor from Nimoy Academy. I was just hired to replace the former head who just met with an unfortunate accident. And I believe the environment that I will bring to our school will make us very competitive with Shatner Middle School.

VERY competitive!"

PHYSICAL BULLYING INCREASES IN ELEMENTARY SCHOOL, PEAKS IN MIDDLE SCHOOL AND DECLINES IN HIGH SCHOOL. VERBAL ABUSE, ON THE OTHER HAND, REMAINS CONSTANT.
— DoSOMETHING.ORG

A Little Bit From BUCK

Here's my guide to some of the terms that are used in this book:

*EPIC FAIL: A loser.

*OFFICIAL: Awesome!

*PWNED (pronounced PONED): In video games it means to completely dominate someone. Like if I said, "I just PWNED you in *Call of Duty*, dude."

It's a really weird word so I looked it up online and found two possible origins:

A map designer for the game *Warcraft* misspelled "owned" and the new word "pwned" was born. The other is basically the same, but it came from a guy playing the game Quake.

*NOOB: A "newbie" pronounced "Noob - ie" Get it?
Someone who is NEW (NOO) to something.

220

KNOWITALL Knows it All!

Okay, so by now you know I love my prefixes. A prefix is placed at the beginning of a word to modify or change its meaning.

You already know about OPTI which has to do with sight.

Here are some others:

ANT or **ANTI**: The Opposite. Against.
ANTagonist: An opponent in a story.
Like Miss Mary was our antagonist.

ANTIbodies: A group of proteins that fight off bad stuff in our bodies. Like when you're sick and you take ANTIbiotics.

ANTIdote: Anything that goes against the effects of poison.

ANTIfreeze: The stuff you put in your car to keep parts of the engine from freezing.

HYPER is another prefix. It means beyond, more than, more than normal

Buck is a bit HYPERactive
Kimmy is a bit HYPERsensitive
Flying into HYPERspace

SUB is another. It means at a lower position or under:
SUBmarine: UNDER water
SUBway: a train that travels UNDER ground
Get it? How many more can you think of?

Chattin' With KIMMY

By now you know that I LOVE chattin' online and blogging. Here are some of my favorite terms.

ROFL   Rolling On the Floor Laughing
AKA   Also Known As
ASAP   As Soon As Possible
B4   Before
BRB   Be Right Back
BTW   By The Way
CYA   See Ya (See You)
IDK   I Don't Know
FYI   For Your Information
GMAB   Give Me A Break
JK   Just Kidding
KK   Okay Kewl (Cool)
L8R   Later (L + eight+ R)
LOL   Laugh Out Loud
SMH   Shaking My Head
TTFN   Ta Ta For Now
TTYL   Talk To You Later
YOLO   You Only Live Once

BOBBY'S Very Limited Knowledge of Being Korean

Okay here are the three things that I learned from my mom's Korean Day Celebration:

Bulgogi: which means "fire meat" in Korean. It's made from thin slices of marinated beef that's flavored with things like soy sauce, sesame oil, garlic, ginger and mushrooms.

Kimchi: a traditional Korean dish made from cabbage.

Hanbok (HAN – BO): a traditional Korean costume.

A Little Bit from Dex

These are some of the Spanish words I use a lot. You know my favorite term is 'sta loca (Esta loca) – That means "it's crazy"

No me importa – It's not important
Muy importante – very important
Tia – Aunt
Abuela – Grandmother
Buenas noches – Good night
Oye – Listen
Esta grande – It's big
Vamanos – Let's go
Por favor, m'ijo (mi hijo) – Please, son
Muy bueno – Very good
Amigos - Friends

And here's a recipe for the breakfast custard that my Grandmother likes to make. It's muy bueno!

Abuela's Maizena (Breakfast custard)

Ingredients
- 2 tablespoons cornstarch
- 1/8 teaspoon salt (that's the smaller one)
- 3 tablespoons white sugar (that's the bigger one)
- 1/8 teaspoon ground cinnamon
- 2 cups whole milk

Directions:
Okay, so first whisk together the cornstarch, salt, sugar, and cinnamon in a large saucepan. (A whisk is one of those wire things that you use to beat eggs with.)

Stir in the milk to evenly blend ingredients, and set over medium-high heat.

Continue whisking and cooking until custard reaches a thick consistency. That should take 25 to 30 minutes.

Es muy importante to stir the entire time, so the custard doesn't burn or clump. If it clumps it's not as good, and the only one who will eat it is Blubber Boy.

The custard will continue to thicken as it cools.

Spoon into bowls to serve.
Enjoy, *amigos!*

About the Authors

Photo Credit Hollis King

Jerry Craft

I am the creator of Mama's Boyz, an award-winning comic strip that has been distributed by King Features Syndicate to close to 900 publications since 1995. My work has earned me five *African American Literary Award Show Open Book Awards.* I've illustrated and / or written more than a dozen children's books, middle-grade books, and graphic novels. In 2014, I saw the release of "The Zero Degree Zombie Zone," a middle grade novel that I illustrated for Scholastic.

This is by far, my longest book, a whopping 228 pages! Which is surprising for someone like me who never thought I could write that much. Plus as a kid, I really didn't like to read, either, so it's funny that I've become an author. But, as I got older, I realized how important it is for people to have stories that they can enjoy, and characters that they can relate to. That's why I do what I do. For more information on my books, upcoming projects, or to book me for school visits, or Skype, feel free to email me at **jerrycraft@aol.com** or visit me on the web at **www.jerrycraft.net**

Plus feel free to write if you just want to talk about the book. Thanks a bunch!!!

Jaylen Craft   Aren Craft

They're not only my sons, but also my co-writers and my focus group. For those of you who don't know what a focus group is, that's when you have an idea or a product and ask a group of people what they think about it. Jaylen (15 years old) and Aren (13) were great when it came to developing characters and also helped to make sure that the story was accurate as far as slang, clothing, texting, video games … For example, they made sure I had Bobby playing Call of Duty games instead of Space Invaders or some other game that I played as a kid.

It's also great to have someone in the house who I can share ideas with whenever I think of them. So what if it's 2 o'clock in the morning and they have school the next day?! Wake up and listen to my idea!

Both boys are huge Xbox fans, like sports, and are Black Belts in Tae Kwon Do. They like to write, and although they don't love to draw the way that I did, they're both starting to get pretty good. Aren did an illustration for my book, *"Who Would Have Thunk It!"* Check my website to see his interview with Drew Pearce, writer of Iron Man 3. Hopefully this will be the first of many that the three of us do together.

the Øffenders

Saving the world while serving detention!

by jerry craft with jaylen craft and aren craft

tell me what you think of this book at jerrycraft@aol.com

Made in the USA
Coppell, TX
30 December 2021

70477168R00129